The Holdfast

Joshua Morgan barely escaped with his life following a bungled bank robbery in Ohio, less than a year after the end of the war between the States. He could not have guessed that he would then find salvation in escorting a tcn-year-old boy across the Indian Nations, in order to return the child to his mother.

The Holdfast

Bill Cartwright

A Black Horse Western

ROBERT HALE

© Bill Cartwright 2019
First published in Great Britain 2019

ISBN 978-0-7198-3067-9

The Crowood Press
The Stable Block
Crowood Lane
Ramsbury
Marlborough
Wiltshire SN8 2HR

www.bhwesterns.com

Robert Hale is an imprint
of The Crowood Press

Typeset by
Derek Doyle & Associates, Shaw Heath
Printed and bound in Great Britain by
4Bind Ltd, Stevenage, SG1 2XT

CHAPTER 1

When the war between the States ended in a crushing and comprehensive defeat for the South, the great majority of those who had fought for the Confederacy accepted the new state of affairs, with varying degrees of reluctance, and returned to their homes to pick up the threads of their lives as best they could. There were those, though, who refused to concede that the war was over, no matter what had been agreed by generals Lee and Grant at Appomattox Courthouse on that beautiful spring day in 1865. These men, who wished to continue fighting the Yankees even after the surrender, were known as diehards or holdfasts.

There is sometimes a very fine line between brigandry and guerrilla warfare. During the war there were those, even in the Confederacy, who maintained that men such as Quantrill and his bushwhackers had regularly crossed this line. Guerrillas had a dubious and uncertain reputation,

5

even among many who were on the same side. The groups who carried on harassing the Union army that was now occupying the southern states needed food and supplies, and these they looted, sometimes from the enemy and at others from civilian establishments such as banks and stores. This led many to view them as a set of ruffians and rascals, rather than noble and quixotic warriors, fighting on for a lost cause.

By the fall of 1865, six months after the surrender, most of the holdfasts had given up and accepted the defeat as a *fait accompli*. But a couple of bands still fought on, one of them a group of seven men in West Virginia who were known to the authorities as the Anderson gang. Calling these guerrilla units 'gangs' was a way of dismissing them as common criminals, rather than treating them as soldiers. The 'Anderson Gang' consisted of two brothers, Bill and Ike Anderson, and five other men. The youngest of these was scarcely old enough to be called a man, being just twenty years of age.

Joshua Morgan had lied about his age and joined the army in Virginia a few days after the shelling of Fort Sumter in April 1861. He was at that time still a couple of weeks shy of his sixteenth birthday. For the next four years the youngster had fought his way across the country, finding himself, when the instrument of surrender was signed, back in his home state of Virginia. Left to himself, he might perhaps have gone home to his ma, whom he had not seen since

6

his last furlough for the Christmas of 1864.

But the unit with which he was then serving had said to a man that they were damned if they were going to take the Ironclad Oath, and so launched a ferocious attack on a nearby Union encampment, whose men had been stood down because their commander believed that the war had ended. In the resulting skirmish, twenty-one Yankees were killed and all but eight of the attacking Confederates also died. Those who remained alive fled from the reinforcements which had been summoned, and went on to form the nucleus of the Anderson Gang.

Now, six months almost to the very day after that action, the Anderson brothers and five of their followers had crossed from Virginia into Ohio, with the intention of robbing the First National Bank of Ohio, which was situated in the town of Oakwood. It was a matter of principle for the group that they would prey only upon Yankee businesses, rather than those where their depredations might cause financial harm to southerners. Crossing over the state line from West Virginia into Ohio like this was typical of their consideration towards those whom they regarded as compatriots.

'You reckon as they'll have any guards there?' asked Morgan. He and the others were seated on their horses on a little hillock overlooking the town. They were about to trot down the slope and then hit the bank immediately.

'I don't look for such,' replied Bill Anderson,

scratching his chin thoughtfully. 'It's not in reason that a little place like this would be expecting robbery.'

His brother Ike was more cautious, saying, 'Whether or no, we need to act like there'll be armed men opposing us. Relax too much and the Lord only knows what'll happen.'

'You allus were a worrier,' said his brother affectionately, 'You're in the right of course, it's better to be careful, but you'll see I'm right.'

As it turned out, Bill Anderson was perfectly correct in his estimation that there would be no armed guards to oppose them when they entered the bank and stole as much cash money as they were able to carry – but for all that the raid was still an unmitigated disaster.

Two groups of riders trotted peaceably down Oakwood's main street, doing their best to look as harmless and inoffensive as possible. True, the men in both parties were armed to the teeth, but that was no uncommon thing in those parts, a matter of months after the end of the war. The first bunch to enter the town consisted of the Andersons, Joshua Morgan and a man called Pete Williams. They were followed a few minutes later by the other three members of the band. When the Andersons reached the premises of the First National Bank of Ohio, they reined in and dismounted, fastening their horses' reins to the hitching rail. Pete Williams and Joshua Morgan followed suit. It would have looked mighty odd to have entered the bank carrying rifles or scatterguns, so the four men just strolled through the door as they were, each one of them carrying no more than a single pistol in a holster.

It was early afternoon and the bank was all but deserted. Two men who looked as though they might be farmers were standing at the counter, chatting amiably with the clerks, and an elderly woman was standing in line behind them, looking as though she was on the verge of becoming impatient at the delay, while the men in front of her chewed the fat.

Outside the bank, the other three men had now fetched up, and as previously agreed, were waiting in the saddle, keeping an eye on what was happening in the street. If anybody who looked like the law showed up by chance, these boys would either deal with him or alert those in the bank to the danger. This method had worked well enough on previous forays into the bank-robbing line. But these men were wholly unprepared when an old woman burst forth from the door of the bank, yelling at the top of her voice, 'It's a robbery! They're a-robbin' of the bank!'

What had happened was that the Anderson brothers had, like the old woman, lost patience with the men gossiping at the counter, and after pulling out their weapons, had announced their intention of taking all the money in the place. So busy had they been covering the farmers and the two clerks that they hadn't thought to set a watch on the old woman, who had bolted for the door before anybody guessed what she was about. There was little to be done about it, though, and the bandits concentrated on encouraging the clerks to stuff a leather satchel with as many bills as they could fit into it.

The residents of that part of Ohio abutting on to Virginia had suffered incursions from irregular forces during the late war, and there was some bitterness about the actions of some of the so-called 'guerrillas', who had killed several local men. While the old woman who had been in the bank was shrieking maledictions and calling down the wrath of God upon those who disturbed in this way the life of a peaceful and law-abiding town like Oakwood, those local citizens who were carrying firearms, which was the majority of the population, began converging purposefully upon the First National Bank of Ohio. Nobody had thought to send word to the sheriff; this was a score which they were content to settle by their own selves. It took no great effort of thought for anybody on Main Street to conclude that those in the bank were most likely holdfasts, looking for an easy source of revenue, and nobody in the town was minded to let them get away easily with their money.

The first intimation of trouble came when those in the bank heard one of their comrades outside call, 'Come on boys, time to go!' This was followed by first one shot and then a perfect fusillade of firing. The man who had shouted the warning at once revealed himself as an accomplice of those robbing the bank and one hot-headed character among those looking to frustrate the robbery of their local bank needed no more excuse than that to open fire, hitting the rider in the back. The shot spooked his mount, who reared up, throwing the man on her back into the dusty roadway. The other two men on horseback went for their guns at this point, but they were hopelessly outnumbered and after a brief exchange of fire, they too were dead.

Those in the bank who heard the shooting outside gauged pretty well what must have happened, and the exultant faces of the bank clerks showed that they too had worked out the play. Bill Anderson pointed his gun straight at the young men behind the mahogany counter and said, 'You fellows just climb over to this side and join us.' The scared bank tellers did as they were bid. Anderson's aim was to use the four townsmen as hostages and bargaining counters, riding off with them on the promise of releasing them later, if there was no pursuit. It was a fatal miscalculation on the part of a man whose instincts in matters of life and death were usually right on the button. Having killed the bandits outside the bank, the crowd outside was in no mood to parlay. Worse, they were trigger happy, ready to shoot at anything and anybody. This was shown when Bill Anderson opened the door to the bank and, gripping his arm hard in order to forestall any attempt at escape, allowed one of the customers who had been in the bank to show himself in the doorway. His idea was to show that they had hostages.

11

It was a bright, sunny day and when the men gathered near the bank saw the door open, they could not see clearly into the shadowy interior. Their blood was up too, which goes some way towards explaining why two or three men took no chances and, anticipating the robbers bursting forth with guns blazing, began shooting at the silhouette in the doorway. Rob Wilson, a hardworking farmer well-known and liked in Oaktown, fell dead with four balls lodged in his chest. After that, things moved with astonishing rapidity.

Realizing, with the death of one of his hostages, that there was no purpose in trying to negotiate, Bill Anderson said to his brother, 'I reckon it's every man for himself, Ike!'

'Reckon you're right,' replied Ike laconically, 'Let's do it then!'

Upon which hint, Bill grabbed the remaining three prisoners and bundled them out of the door ahead of them, trying as far as possible to use them as shields. There were a couple of shots from the men outside, before somebody yelled, 'Hold your fire! That's the boys from the bank.'

The terrified bank tellers were blinking in the sunlight, with the four robbers crouching behind them, urging them on towards where the horses were tethered. A breathless hush descended upon the crowd outside the bank, for nobody wished to be the one who precipitated a general bloodbath. For a second or two it looked as if the men who had tried to raid the bank might just have got away with it, until one of the men with their guns trained upon them and their hostages found that he had a clear and unobstructed line of fire at one of the bandits. Without thinking further, he took his shot, killing Ike Anderson stone dead – whereupon all hell broke loose.

Seeing his brother's head pop open at the back like an over-ripe melon, Bill Anderson was overwhelmed by a killing rage, which caused him to forget all about escaping and instead to concentrate on slaughtering as many people as possible in the time remaining to him. He began by shooting one of the bank tellers and then ran at top speed towards the ring of men encircling the bank, firing as he went. For a moment, those whom he was charging at were too taken aback to respond, but then every gun was trained on the charging madman, and he was struck by a couple of dozen shots.

Anderson's mad and suicidal dash served temporarily to distract attention from the two remaining robbers, who took the opportunity to free their mounts and vault into the saddle. Once mounted, Pete Williams could not prevent himself from sending a few balls whistling towards the townsfolk, drawing an instant response in the form of a withering fire directed at him and his horse. The smoke from this and the earlier firing at Bill Anderson obscured the sight a little of the furious men and allowed Josh Morgan, who alone seemed to have no interest in killing anybody that day, to jab his spurs viciously in the mare's flanks, causing the beast to fly like an arrow from a bow, down Main Street towards the edge of town. He would never have had a chance had it not been for the madness that had seized both his former comrades and their adversaries, and made them more intent upon killing each other than in working through the possibilities of the situation in a rational and clearheaded fashion.

Be that as it may, Joshua Morgan galloped away down the road leading out of town, and by the time that those in the town had recollected themselves and discovered that one of the men concerned in the robbery had made off, there was little to be done about it, beyond firing wild shots after a target that was by now vanishing out of range of the attackers. It might have been a different story had anybody been carrying a rifle that day, but firing pistols at a fast-moving target, over a hundred yards away, is an enterprise not often apt to be crowned with success.

For better than ten minutes, Morgan maintained as furious a pace as could be managed, putting some four miles between him and the scene of the recent catastrophe. At length he slowed, first to a canter and then a gentle trot. His mind was working frantically, trying to make some sense of what had happened. One fact stood out starkly: for the first time since he had joined the army, four and a half years ago, he was now altogether alone and wholly reliant upon his own resources. It was an unnerving thought. He wondered whether or not his honour should have required him to die back in Oakwood with his friends and former comrades in arms, but he could think that it did not: this was surely one of those occasions when it is a case of every man for himself. Besides which, by the time he had dug up and left the town in such haste, everybody else seemed to have been killed. Leastways, so he suspected. Although he had not actually seen Williams die, it seemed likely enough that he had gone down the same road as the Anderson brothers and the three men who had been setting watch outside the bank. It was the hell of a business.

Morgan wanted to give the horse a little rest before putting even more distance between himself and the town. There was a very real chance that after what had happened, some man with a great sense of civic responsibility might try and put together a posse and ride in pursuit of the sole survivor of the abortive bank robbery. He had seen one of the men from the bank gunned down by Bill Anderson, just before he in turn was killed, and an episode like that, where some innocent party ended up dead, was just the kind of incident that tended to arouse the wrath of men who were just minding their own business and living quietly. Josh Morgan also doubted that if and when such a body of vengeance seekers were to catch up with him, there would be any sort of trial: they would almost certainly just string him up from the nearest tree.

It was while he was musing in this way about his future prospects that Joshua Morgan heard two sounds, one following on swiftly from the other. The first was a child's high and desperate voice crying out, 'Help!' The second was a deep growl, so deep and low that he could not at first make out what it might be. Then it dawned on him that it was an animal, and combined with that terrified appeal for aid, he figured that some child was in danger of being attacked. He tried to get the mare to move towards the sounds, but she was seriously spooked and jittered from side to side, unwilling to go off the track and into the trees from whence the sounds had come. This was a horse that would endure heavy gunfire with equanimity, and so whatever it was that was scaring her must be something quite formidable.

There came another cry, this one an octave or so higher than the first. It was impossible to gauge whether a boy or girl had made the wordless sound. Morgan jumped down from the saddle and ran through the undergrowth and trees to see what was happening. He did not have far to go, for in a little clearing, no more than twenty-five yards from the track, he stumbled upon a horrifying scene. A boy, who could have been no more than eleven years of age, was standing with his back against a tree. By the look of him, he was paralysed with fear, and if

Morgan was any judge of such things, on the point of fainting. Given his situation, Josh Morgan didn't blame him one little bit, for in front of the child and ten feet or so from him, an enormous black bear was standing on its hind legs, towering over the little boy and growling angrily.

Away over to his left, Morgan caught a glimpse of a bear cub, and it was easy enough to see what had happened: this was a she-bear, protecting her cub from what she apprehended to be a threat. It was a shame, but there was nothing for it but to kill this fine animal and that right speedily, before she lunged at the child and tore his head from his body. Morgan waved his arms and shouted, to distract the bear's attention from the boy and almost became a victim himself, for the creature whirled round, dropped on to all fours and charged him. He scarcely had time to pull out his pistol and begin firing at the bear's slavering jaws.

It was a damned close-run thing, for it was only on the fifth and final shot that the bear first halted and then dropped to the forest floor. It came to rest only a few feet from Morgan, who found that his heart was pounding like a steam hammer. He had seen his share of dangerous situations, but truly believed that he had come closer to death that day than at any time during the war.

The boy had not, contrary to Josh Morgan's expectations, passed out, and remained standing by the tree, breathing heavily. Morgan went over to him and

17

said, 'You're white as a hant. Sit down and lean your head between your knees or you're like to pass out.'

The boy did as he was told and sat in that position for a few seconds. He hated to hurry someone of such tender years who had been through such a terrifying experience, but Morgan was keenly aware that even at that very moment, a body of armed men might be riding towards them with the notion of stretching his neck. He said, 'Where's your ma?'

'At home, I guess.'

'Where might that be?'

'Jubilee. In Texas, you know.'

'Texas!' exclaimed Morgan in amazement, 'Lord a mercy, that's more'n a thousand miles from here. What about your pa?'

'He was promoted to glory this year.'

'Well how'd you get here? You got kin nearby?'

The child sat up and stared at Morgan. He said, 'I been living with my grandpapa, but I left him now.'

The bear cub had come over and had begun nuzzling at its mother's lifeless body. If it had not been for the desperate straits in which he found himself, Morgan might have felt sorry for the critter. As it was, he said, 'Well, I can't leave you here on your own. Where's this grandpapa of yours live?'

The child gestured in the general direction in which Morgan had already been travelling, for which he was heartily thankful. The idea of heading back towards Oaktown was a peculiarly uninviting one. He said, 'You best come with me now and I'll take you to where you're staying.'

Once he had the boy up on the saddle in front of him, Morgan set the mare going at a brisk trot. He had already lost more time than was comfortable, given the circumstances in which he was placed. There was some mystery here, but he surely didn't have time to unravel it. What on earth could the child mean when he said that he had left his grandfather, and what was he doing a thousand miles from his mother? These matters were no affair of his, though, and he would be fulfilling his Christian duty if he simply delivered the boy to safety.

Once they emerged from the little wood through which they had been passing, Morgan could see a neat patchwork of fields before him. They rode for a while in silence. He said to the boy, 'Did you walk all this way by yourself?'

'Yes, I want to go home to my ma.'

'But you're staying with your grandpa, is that it?'

The child nodded miserably and said, 'But I want to go home.'

After another half hour, they came in sight of a huge, stone-built house, which put Morgan in mind of some of the plantation houses in the south. Beautiful grounds surrounded this mansion, and it was clearly the home of somebody of great consequence. To his surprise, the boy said, 'That's my grandpa's house.'

'The devil it is,' muttered Morgan. 'He must be a wealthy enough sort of fellow from the look of it.'

As they rode up the drive leading to the grand property, Morgan noticed uneasily that the place was a regular hive of activity, with men mounting up and people shouting instructions. If it were not for the fact that they had been travelling on the only track from Oakwood to this place, and nobody had overtaken them, he might have been affeared that word had reached the inhabitants here about the raid on Oaktown, and that these men were forming a posse. There were a dozen men in front of the house, some toting rifles and all looking serious and determined. When they caught sight of Morgan and his young charge, there were cries of recognition and some of the men came running towards them. It was Joshua Morgan's impression that although they seemed pleased to see the boy, these men were eying him unfavourably.

While Josh Morgan was wondering how matters would pan out, the small crowd of men parted, allowing an old man to stump forward with the aid of a cane. Apart from his limp, the old fellow looked hale enough, and when he spoke, his voice was as powerful as any youngster. He said sharply, 'All right, boy's been found. Safe and sound by the look of him, too. You men have work to do.' When those gathered around made no move, he raised his voice and practically yelled at them, 'Go on. Leave me be. I want to speak to this youngster.'

After the men drifted away, a few of them grumbling and casting puzzled looks towards Morgan and the child, the old man came up and said irritably, 'Come on then, get down. Let me see that my grand-son's safe.'

After dismounting, Morgan lifted down the little boy. His grandfather reached out to tussle the child's hair, but the boy flinched away from him. 'What got into your head, Tommy?' asked the old man, 'Why ever d'you wander off like that? I was plumb dis-tracted when I found you were lost.' There was no reply to these questions.

Turning to Morgan, the man said, 'How'd you find him, son?'

Briefly, Morgan gave an account of coming across the boy being menaced by the bear.

'Black bear, hey? I didn't even know there were any such round these parts any more.'

'Sometimes they swim across the river from Kentucky. I heard so, anyways.'

'Well then, it was a long way from home. So you saved the boy's life, hey? I'm thankful for it, more than you can know.'

At that moment, both men looked round, because there was a thunder of many hoofs. Fifteen or twenty riders were galloping down on them. These men were grim-faced and heavily armed. Morgan thought that they had the look not of cowboys, but rather ordinary citizens who have jumped on a horse in a hurry to perform some urgent quest. Without the shadow of a doubt, this was the posse whose arrival he had dreaded. Unless he was greatly mistaken, thought Morgan, the life remaining to him could now be measured in minutes, rather than years or decades.

CHAPTER 2

The men reined in and every one of them was staring hard at Joshua Morgan. The old man at his side said, 'Well, what can I do for you boys? Jack, what brings you out this way?'

The rider thus addressed said, 'Sorry to be troubling you, Mister Walters, but that there young man was mixed up in a shooting over in Oakwood. There's four men killed dead and we come for to take him back to face justice.'

The man they called Walters chuckled and then recollected himself, saying, 'I'm sorry, I shouldn't laugh. What you tell me is terrible, just terrible. Still, this ain't the fellow you're after. This boy works for me. He hasn't set foot off my property all day, so I don't see how he could have been robbing banks over in Oakwood.'

A dead silence followed this declaration. It was tolerably plain to Joshua Morgan that some of those men in the posse recognized him and knew for certain sure that he was one of the bandits. The man called Jack had fixed Morgan with no friendly eye and said, 'Begging your pardon sir, but I don't rightly see how that can be. We tracked this young villain here, and I saw him at Oakwood with my own eyes.'

The old man's voice dropped until it was little more than a whisper. He was evidently not accustomed to having his word questioned. He said softly, 'You calling me a liar, Jack?'

'Nothing o' the sort, Mister Walters. Happen, though, that you might have made an error. . . .'

'I don't know that saying I'm going senile and losing my memory is any better than telling me to my face that I'm a liar.'

There was a long silence. At last the old man said, 'You fellows might not have work to do, but me and my boys surely have. If there's nothing more, I'll be bidding you a good day.'

The rider to whom he had been talking gave one last look at Joshua Morgan, as though hoping to imprint that young man's face upon his memory, then without another word, he wheeled his horse round and set off back towards town. The other men followed him. Morgan, the old man and the boy stood there without speaking until the sound of the hoofbeats had faded and died. Then the younger man said, 'I reckon as I owe you my life, sir.'

'Huh, I always pay my debts. You think I would have been such a cur as to let them take you off and lynch you, after you saved my own flesh and blood and delivered him safe home to me?'

Neither then, nor later, did Josh Morgan ever discover what hold Jacob Walters had over the people of Oakwood. Once he said that he owned the town, and on another occasion he claimed to have founded the place and been responsible for building most of it. What was plain was that nobody in that town would ever dare to cross the old man.

'Well sir, I reckon I'll be off now,' said Morgan, 'I'm glad I was there to protect your grandson.'

'Not so hasty. You don't think that you'll be able to leave here in a hurry? Why, if you've the sense the good Lord gave a goat, you'll know that those men'll be prowling around the edge of my land to see if they can catch you when I'm not around.'

'The thought had crossed my mind,' admitted Morgan, 'But we're quits now and you don't owe me a thing.'

'You're a stiff-necked devil,' said Walters, but not in such a way as to indicate that he disapproved of such a character. 'I can see you're proud as Lucifer, and you'd rather be hanged than be beholden to anybody. Well, I won't have it. You can bunk down here for a few days, and then leave when we're sure that it's safe.'

Something else that Morgan noticed later was that at no time did old Mister Walters ask if he actually *had* been tied up in any shooting at Oakwood. It was enough for him that his grandson had been saved from harm. That night, Morgan was given a cot in one of the bunkhouses that housed the workers on Jacob Walters' land. The other men were polite enough, but a little wary, as though they couldn't quite calculate where Morgan fitted into things. However, it was easier the next morning, when some of the men began operating a forge: Morgan had had quite a little experience of smithing during the war, and so he offered to lend a hand.

After an hour or two, the others lost their reserve, and although he would not be drawn into discussing why the posse had been trailing him, they all chatted amiably. While they were resting and having coffee, one of the men nudged Morgan and said, 'You got a friend there and no mistake.' Looking over to where the man had gestured, he saw that the boy was standing there, watching him.

'It's Tom, isn't it?' asked Morgan. 'You want to join us?' Shyly, the youngster came over to where the three men were lounging. Morgan said, 'You want some coffee?'

He'd never had much dealings with children, but for some reason, he found it easy to get on with this lad. Tom came over and sat next to Morgan and accept a tin cup of coffee. 'You don't go to school?'

'Got a tutor.'

'I don't see him about,' remarked Morgan. Then he twigged and said, 'Ah, you're playing hooky, is that it?'

For the first time that he had known him, the boy actually smiled. Morgan said to the others, 'Listen,

I'll be back directly. I better let somebody know that this young rascal ain't gone missing again.'

By the time that the two of them got back to the big house, the alarm had already been raised, and when he knocked on the door, Morgan found that Jacob Walters was in the middle of a furious disputation with a pale and weedy-looking man in his middle years, who was presumably the tutor. As they had walked across from the forge, Tommy had slipped his hand trustingly into Morgan's, and so when Walters became aware of them, he saw immediately that they were standing there hand in hand. He stared hard at this spectacle for a space, before saying curtly to the tutor. 'You're discharged. You can have a month's money, but just clear out of here. You're as much use as . . .' the old man was seemingly about to come out with a vulgar simile, but stopped himself in time and remembered that a child of tender years was present, and he said instead, 'As much use as nothing. Go on, be off with you.'

Morgan was about to slip away and get back to the smithy, but Jacob Walters said sharply, 'I don't know where you're off to, but I want you in my study. Come on.'

Before following the master of the house, Morgan said to Tommy, 'Will you promise not to run off and get lost while I talk with your grandpa?'

'I promise.'

This exchange was heard by Walters, who glanced back over his shoulder with an inscrutable expression on his wrinkled countenance. When the two men were in Walters' sanctum, which was comfortably furnished and served both as study and library, the old man invited Morgan to take a seat in a plush armchair. He said, 'The boy's fond of you. That's the first time I ever knew him to take anybody's hand.'

'He's a nice little fellow.'

'Let's come to the point. You're running from something. I don't ask what, for I don't much care. But I can see that you're a decent young man.'

Unable to see where all this was tending, Joshua Morgan remained quiet and waited to see what would follow. He almost fell off the chair in astonishment when Jacob Walters said, 'How'd you like the job of taking care of Tommy?'

'I reckon you have me pegged for somebody else,' replied Morgan, smiling, 'I've no book-learning to speak of. You looking for a tutor or teacher for the boy, you'd best look elsewhere.'

'Teacher be damned. I want somebody that he likes and trusts. Somebody as can take care of him, stop him running off, and maybe help if anybody tries to snatch him away. You strike me as a handy fellow for that kind of work.'

Once again, Morgan felt that he was on the fringe of some mystery. The boy had been running away from his grandpa when they met, and he had seen how he had shrunk away from the touch of his grandfather's hand, as though he was afraid of him. He said, 'Why should Tommy run off from here? And where's his ma?'

Old Mister Walters looked at Morgan incredulously. He couldn't trust himself to speak, but his face went pink with fury. At last he said, 'You dare ask me such questions?'

'I reckon so,' replied Morgan imperturbably, 'You're asking me to take a job, and I want to know what's what. It all sounds odd. Why would you engage somebody like me, a stranger, to look after the child, when you've enough money to hire a squad of Pinkertons men if you wanted the business done securely? It doesn't make sense.'

After this little speech the young man half expected to be thrown out on his ear, but Jacob Walters seemed to want something from him and so was prepared to allow Morgan some licence. It was a novelty for Walters to meet a man who did not kowtow to him and abase himself for fear of causing offence. Something about the set-up tickled the old man's fancy, for he said, 'You've a rare nerve boy, I'll give you that! As for Pinkertons, well, I'm not in their good books, so I couldn't use 'em even if I wanted to. But I've something else in mind. I want you to take the boy around with you, talk to him, maybe teach him to be a little more manly. He grew up surrounded by women, and it shows. 'Sides which, he's taken to you.'

'You take oath that you really are his grandpa, and that this is all above board?'

For a moment it looked once more as though Walters was about to erupt in fury, but he subsided again and gave his word that the case was as he represented it. Upon which, Joshua Morgan said, 'All right, Mister Walters. I'll do it.'

There then began the strangest period of Josh Morgan's young life: he became, to all intents and purposes, a nursemaid. This was such an improbable and unlooked for development that he could hardly believe himself that it was true. Nevertheless, for the next five weeks he looked after Tommy Walters, who was apparently a month or two short of his eleventh birthday, from morning 'til nightfall. The two of them explored the land that his grandfather owned, and whenever the boy expressed any interest, whether in the life cycle of frogs, the catching of fish, or how a cap and ball pistol worked, Josh Morgan did his best to explain, and illustrated his lessons with practical demonstrations. Mister Walters hadn't entirely given up on the more academic side of the boy's education, but felt that it could perhaps be delayed for a few months, until the pupil was more willing to cooperate.

To begin with, the whole arrangement was so peculiar that it served to take Morgan's mind from the awful fact that his friends and companions had all been killed in front of him. He had fought with those men as soldiers and then ridden with them as outlaws, and they'd been the closest thing he had to family. Finding himself cut off from them so abruptly felt almost like a bereavement. Still, there it was. He was young and healthy and had escaped with his own life, which at one point had not seemed likely. His sorrow at the loss of his comrades was softened and ameliorated by the fact that he was himself still in the land of the living.

There was also the undeniable circumstance that he was beginning to doubt that his own view of matters since the end of the war was the only correct one. After Tommy was in bed, and thank the Lord that there was a real maid to see to such things, Morgan took to wandering down to the bunkhouses and chatting to the boys who lived there. At first they had been a little reserved with him, not quite understanding how he fitted into the scheme of things on Jacob Walters' estate, but they soon found him an open and agreeable young man, and relaxed in his company.

Having been for the last six months or so almost exclusively in the company of holdfasts, it was something of a revelation to observe that everybody else had long since decided that the war was over and that there was nothing to be done now but to get on with life as best one could. Among the workers were both former Confederates and men who had fought on the opposite side, but they all rubbed along well enough on the whole. The bitterness that he had encountered daily in the Anderson gang was altogether absent. It felt distinctly strange to sit down at table with Yankees who had, until a few short months earlier, been soldiers in the Union army, but then again, they ate the same food as anybody else and had the same fears and desires as anybody from the South. It took a little getting used to, but get used to it he did.

One of Morgan's duties was to report each day to Walters how things were going with his grandson. This, too, struck Morgan at first as a strange business, but it was only later that he realized that Tommy would hardly ever speak a single word of his own volition to his grandfather. What the source of this animosity was, he had no idea at all. From odd remarks that his young charge let drop, Morgan gathered that the youngster had left his mother suddenly and unexpectedly, and that his one wish was to go home again. He behaved almost like a captive, a prisoner of war or something of that kind. It was all most perplexing. But the answer to the riddle came on a chilly November morning, when, in the middle of explaining to Tommy how and why a blacksmith needs to heat a piece of metal red-hot before it can be worked, one of the servants from the house came hurrying up and said in a low voice, 'Boss wants to see you.'

'Can it wait, d'you think? We're kind o' busy here.'

'No, it's real urgent.'

'Oh well, I guess your master will have his way.' Morgan turned to the boy and said, 'Tommy, can I trust you not to get into mischief while I'm gone?'

'We'll set a watch on him,' volunteered one of the men working in the smithy, 'He'll be safe here with us, Morgan.'

To his surprise, the servant led Morgan not to the study, where he was usually interviewed by his employer, but up the broad, carpeted staircase that led to the two upper storeys of the house. He had never been upstairs at the big house, and wondered what the idea was. After leading Morgan along a long corridor, the man stopped at a door and knocked softly, before opening it without waiting for an invitation to enter. Inside, in a large double bed, lay Jacob Walters.

Morgan was no sawbones, but it was as plain as the nose on his face that here was a man who had not long to live. Walters' face was almost as white as the sheets and pillows on which he lay, and one side of his stern countenance was weirdly contorted, as though the muscles on the left side of his face were no longer working. When the old man spoke, his speech, too, was distorted and faint. Without waiting to be told, the servant who had conducted him here left the room quietly, closing the door noiselessly behind him.

'I'm sorry to see you laid low in this way, sir. . . .' began Morgan conventionally, but Walters cut in impatiently. His voice was reedy and thin, but the iron will that drove him was still present.

'Never mind that nonsense. I'm dying. I need your aid.'

'I'd think a doctor or priest would be more use to you than I'm apt to be.'

'Never mind what you think. Just listen.' The old

man was gasping for breath, and clearly wished to get out what he had to say before the effort exhausted him. He said: 'Had the first seizure six months ago. That's when I came up with the idea. But it was a bad thing I did, and you're the one to set it straight.'

'You been good to me, Mister Jacobs,' said Morgan slowly, 'Fact is, I owe my life to you. I'll help how I can.'

'Well then, take a seat there. I can't be doing with a body looming over me like that.'

When Josh Morgan had pulled a chair over to the bedside, Walters began talking. He said, 'I was a poor father. Had but one son and his mother died in childbirth. Happen I blamed him for my wife's death, but whatever it was, I was cold and strict. First chance he had, the boy lit out, ran away south and married. Truth to tell, I was glad to be rid of him, never mind that he was no older than you are now.'

It was not easy to see where all this was leading, and so Morgan said nothing.

'As the years rolled by, I missed him and wanted to make amends, but had no idea where he was to be found. I never heard of him again until this April just gone. Piece in the newspaper gave his name as being killed at the Battle of West Point, just before the sur-render.' The old man was suddenly racked with a fit of coughing, which left his face glistening with sweat. Morgan made as though to rise and fetch help, but Jacob Walters' eye caught and held him. It was obvious that he wanted neither help nor interruption until he'd finished his tale.

'The newspaper mentioned that my son left a widow and young son right up in the Texas panhandle. I hired Pinkertons' men to track them down.'

'What for?'

'That boy of his was my only living kin. I wanted him here with me. I thought maybe ... maybe I could. . . .'

Morgan shook his head sadly as he saw just what the old man had had in mind. He said, 'You thought that you could raise Tommy and be a loving father to him and make up for how you'd been with his father, when he was a young 'un.'

'Pretty much.'

'What did the child's ma have to say about the scheme? I can't see any mother being fired up about an idea like that.'

'I didn't consult her.'

It took a moment for the implications of this blunt statement to sink in, and when they did, Joshua Morgan gasped with disbelief. He exclaimed, 'Lord 'a mercy, don't tell me you had the boy snatched from his mother?'

'I did. When Pinkertons had found where he and his ma were living, I hired some roughnecks to go down there and steal the boy away and bring him here.'

'God almighty,' cried Joshua Morgan, genuinely shocked, 'I never heard the like! What can you have been thinking?'

'Well, you seen the consequence of it. The boy all but hates me. He shrinks away from my touch, as though I were a leper or something.'

'Don't know as I blame him, to speak plainly.'

'I'm dying. I need no doctor to tell me so. Will you help me set things right?'

Morgan rubbed his chin thoughtfully and looked at the old man in the bed, who looked a good deal less fearsome than usual. He said, 'What would you have me do?'

'Take the boy back to his mother. Will you do it?'

'Like I say, you've been mighty good to me, sir. You saved my life and set me on my feet. Besides which, that child being separated from his mother like that, well that's a wrong to be set straight. I'll do it.'

Jacob Walters looked as though he was relaxing slightly, but he wished first to make sure of matters. He said to the young man, 'You give your oath on it?'

'I promise I'll do it or die in the attempt.'

'My man's saddling up your horse this minute and doing the same for Tommy's pony. He's putting enough gold in your saddle-bag too, to pay for the journey. I always felt you were a man I could trust, soon as I laid eyes on you. He's putting papers that will show Tommy's home and how to get to it, too. You know he'll inherit all this place when I die?'

'That's none of my affair. You want I should bring your grandson here, to bid you farewell?'

Jacob Walters sighed and looked very sad. He said, 'I declare, the boy hates the sight of me. If he'll come, then yes, I'd be glad to say goodbye. But don't force him. The sooner I know that he's on his way back to his mother, the easier I'll rest.'

Back at the smithy, the men were showing Tommy how to quench hot metal in water, to harden it. Morgan said to the boy, 'I'd like the pleasure of a quiet word, if you will.' When they were out of earshot of the others, he continued, 'Your grandfather has charged me to take you home, son. What do you say to that?'

'Truly? You ain't funning with me?'

'Not a bit of it. But I want something from you in return.'

'Anything at all, sir,' said Tommy, his eyes shining with pleasurable anticipation.

'Well then, it's this. Your grandpa's very ill. . . .'

Before he could say any more, the child cut in fiercely, saying, 'I'm glad! I hate him.'

'That's not the way to talk. He's your kin. He told me somewhat of your story and I'll be the first to own that he acted wrongly. He knows that now. Come, will you not just say goodbye to him pleasantly? It would ease his mind.'

Tommy looked as though he was torn between his wish to oblige the man to whom he had taken such a liking, and a desire to express his hostility towards the old man who had caused him to be snatched from his mother. He didn't speak for a few seconds, but finally said, 'If you like, I'll say farewell to him, but only 'cause you want it.'

'Stout fellow. Let's go and do it directly, then we can be on our way.'

Even in the few minutes that had elapsed between leaving the old man's sickbed and returning with his grandson, it seemed to Morgan that the patient's condition had noticeably worsened, although that could, of course, have been his imagination. He didn't think so, though. He was sure that Walters' breathing was more laboured and his eyes less alert than when they had talked earlier. Morgan said, 'Your grandson would say goodbye to you, sir, and tell that he forgives you for what was done.' This went considerably beyond what Tommy had agreed to before they had come to the room, and he shot Morgan a look. Jacob Walters said, with palpable relief in his voice, 'You forgive me, boy? It's a heavy burden lifted from my shoulders. A heavy burden.'

Tommy glanced across to Morgan, who nodded his head slightly to indicate that the boy should accede to this request. Walters' grandson said, 'Yes sir, I do.' Then, unprompted, he leaned over and kissed the dying man's cheek. Although Morgan knew that this was all being done as a favour, to please him, he was relieved, and hoped that the old man might now die in peace.

After they left the room and were moving down the stairs, the boy muttered softly, 'I still hate him, for all that.'

'Well then, you did the right thing anyway, and that's a mercy. Let's get on over to the stables and see if those mounts are ready. We got a long journey ahead of us, I guess you realize that?'

'Are we going to ride the whole way?'

'Lord help you, no! We'd be lucky to hit Texas this side of Christmas. No, your grandpa says that he's given me money to pay for our little jaunt. We can take a railroad train for the chief of the distance and then ride from stop to stop, where it's needful.'

When they reached the foot of the staircase, Tommy Walters stopped and then turned to Morgan, saying, 'Did you like my grandpa?'

Morgan considered the question thoughtfully, as though it had been posed by an adult and not a young child. At length, he replied, 'No, I wouldn't precisely say that I liked him. More I respected him. I owe him a great debt, too, and want to repay it.'

'You owe my grandfather a heap of money?'

'There's other debts, 'sides those that involve cash money.'

Just as he had been told, the horses were both saddled up and ready to go, but Joshua Morgan wanted to double-check everything before embarking upon such a long journey, and with the additional duty of caring for somebody else's child the while. This was a novelty for him. Morgan was used to caring for his own self and also guarding the interests of various comrades, but the notion of being solely responsible for the welfare of some other person was a strange one, and he wasn't yet sure how he felt about it.

In the saddle bag Morgan found a little leather pouch containing fifteen gold, double eagle $20 pieces – more than enough to see the two of them safe to Texas and with a little to spare. Already his thoughts were turning towards the best route, and even what he might do when once he had delivered himself of his young charge. Well, as scripture had it: 'Sufficient unto the day is the evil thereof.' There would be time to fret about what he was going to do with his life when he had fulfilled his promise to the dying man. Morgan said to the boy waiting at his side: 'Well, you ready to go?'

'Yes, sir.'

'There's no "sir" in the case, son. Just call me Josh or Morgan, if you will. Anything else makes me feel real old.'

CHAPTER 3

So pleasantly had the last few weeks passed that
Joshua Morgan had, almost incredibly to relate, all
but forgotten about the unfortunate affair at
Oakwood. It was not, after all, the first gun battle in
which he had been caught up, and since he had
himself not fired a single shot on this occasion, he
felt that he could, with justice to himself, count the
matter as over and done with. However, there were
those who held quite the opposite view of the case.

Once they had accepted him as a regular kind of
fellow and essentially one of them, the other hands
on the Walters' place took care to keep Morgan
informed of any interest in him that they heard when
visiting town. Most of the other men living in the
bunkhouses had pasts that might not have borne
close examination, and so the fact that the new hand
had left Oakwood one step ahead of a necktie party
by no means prejudiced them against him. A week
after he arrived at Jacob Walters' ranch, one of the

41

other men returned from town and sought Morgan out at once. An interesting circumstance was that this man had been in the Yankee army, but even knowing that Morgan was a southerner did not prevent him from giving a quiet warning. He said, 'I don't know what's what, but you're the talk of the town over in Oakwood. I shouldn't set foot off this place, were I you.' Morgan had thanked the man heartily, only to be told, 'Well, we all got to stick together.' The idea of his 'sticking together' with a former Yankee soldier was a strange one.

By some means or other, probably because the Anderson Gang had been so notorious, Morgan's name was now known in town. Furthermore the name 'Joshua Morgan' was now being voiced abroad in Oakwood, another of the men told him one night. He asked nothing about Morgan's past, but advised him to be exceedingly careful if ever he left the place.

One might have thought that these warnings would have preyed on Joshua Morgan's mind as he and the boy trotted out of Jacob Walters' estate and took the road west. As it happened, he was so preoccupied with planning the journey and chatting amiably to the child riding beside him that he thought nothing of it when two mean-looking men rode up on them from the opposite direction, after they had been on the road for fifteen minutes or so. It was not until one of the riders was almost upon them and Morgan was encouraging Tommy to move to one side, that one of the men manoeuvred his mount so that it was blocking their way. At the same time, one man pulled a pistol and the other drew a sawn-off scattergun from a scabbard at front of the saddle. They both drew down on Morgan and one of them said, 'Get down off o' your horse.'

'Is this a shakedown? I've a child to care for, have some pity.'

'You think we're a robbin' of you?' asked one of the men, a hulking, ill-favoured fellow with a mean and cunning countenance. 'Not a bit of it. There's a price on your head. I reckon you be Joshua Morgan.'

'You're bounty men?' exclaimed Morgan, unable to avoid showing the detestation that he felt for such types. 'You'd sell me for money?'

The man with the scattergun kept it trained on Morgan, and in the process, partly aimed at Tommy Walters. While this was the situation, Morgan dared not risk a violent confrontation, for the child would be sure to get caught in the crossfire.

'That's enough talk,' said the man with the pistol, 'Get down.' As he spoke, he dismounted himself, all the while keeping a close eye on Morgan, who saw no point in doing other than he was bid.

Once Morgan and the man who supposed himself to be capturing him were on the ground, the bounty hunter said, 'Take out that pistol o' your'n, but as slow as you like. Reward on you's dead or alive, but I'd as soon not have to cart a corpse round. Easier on us all if you can ride. Draw it out by the trigger guard, just with one finger. Don't you so much as touch the hilts of it.'

This instruction told Joshua Morgan all he needed to know about these men, namely that they were not seasoned bounty men at all, and most likely this was their first essay into the field. From all that Morgan was able to apprehend, it was also apt to be their last. Very slowly and delicately, he reached down to the holster and hooked his forefinger through the trigger guard of the Colt Army that nestled there. Then, still moving with exaggerated slowness, he lifted it up and offered it to the man standing in front of him, who must by now have thought that everything was going just fine and dandy.

Morgan stretched out his arm with the apparent intention of handing over his weapon to the man standing triumphantly in front of him. The pistol swung free from his finger, the balance of it causing the barrel to angle back towards Morgan. As the other reached out his hand, a quick flick of Morgan's wrist rotated the gun, bringing the hilts up into his palm. As his fingers closed, gripping it securely, Morgan's thumb cocked the piece and he fired almost as soon as the hammer locked in place, the ball taking the other man just below his collar bone.

Without pausing to see what was what, Morgan followed this first shot by whirling round and firing a couple of times at the rider with the shotgun.

Tommy, still seated on his pony, was safely out of line of any but the wildest and most reckless shooting.

He watched in astonishment as Morgan, having fired just three shots, strode forwards to kick away the gun in the hand of the man now laying flat on his back in the roadway. He turned, cocking his pistol once more, at a sound behind him, but it was only the scattergun-wielding man whom he had shot twice, slipping from the saddle and crashing to the earth.

All these events took place with the greatest speed, and by the time the boy had caught his breath and was ready to be alarmed or distressed, it was all over and there was complete silence. At first he thought that his friend Joshua had killed both of the men, but then he saw that the one on his back, the first person to be shot, had his eyes open and was trying to sit up. Tommy watched, horrified and yet at the same time fascinated, to see what would happen next. What happened was that Morgan squatted down by the man's head and spoke quietly to him. Blood was leaking freely from the wound, the ball having taken him in the chest, on his left side.

Morgan said, 'I don't think you're going to recover from that.'

The other man tried to smile, but his expression changed and became a twisted rictus of pain as he breathed in. He waited for the agony to subside a little, and then replied: 'I dursn't look. Is it through my lung?'

'Yes,' said Morgan, seeing little point in prevaricating, 'From the colour of the blood, I'd say so.'

'Well then, it's all up with me.'

'I reckon so.'

Tommy Walters could not for the life of him imagine how it was possible for people to talk in this way about death. Knowing that his grandfather was dying had been different. He was an old man, and in any case, Tommy had not been overly fond of him. This was a different thing entirely. A moment or two earlier, this had been an active and vigorous man in full possession of his strength. Now, he had been brought low and was at the point of death. The sudden reverse was disturbing, and he continued to observe the scene, wondering what would next happen. It was rather an anti-climax when Morgan got to his feet and announced quietly, 'We'd best be getting on.'

'What about. . . .'

'Those fellows? They're both dead. There's naught we can do for them.'

'You'd leave them here? What about burying them and such?'

'Son,' explained Morgan gently, 'if we don't get on, then there might be friends of those men hereabouts, or somebody else with a similar notion, which is to say, taking me prisoner. What would become of you then? I made a promise to your grandpapa and I mean to keep it.'

For a good five minutes after starting off down the road again, Tommy Walters was silent. Then he asked, 'What happened back there?'

'I killed two men, is what happened,' replied

Morgan soberly, 'It's the hell of a thing.'

'No, I mean how did you do it? One minute there's two of 'em with their guns on you, and next thing, you shot them both.'

'Oh, that! I knew the pair of them were rank amateurs the moment I was told to pull out my pistol by hooking a finger through the trigger guard. Anybody with experience in such matters would've have me lift it from the holster by gripping the hilts with my thumb and forefinger.'

'Why's that, sir? I mean Joshua.'

'You saw what resulted. It's an old, old trick. Some call it the road agent's spin, others the Missouri roll. Once you got your gun held like that, you need only flick your hand and the hilts come up and you can grip it like normal. Those boys wasn't going to last long in the bounty game, not if they didn't even know something like that. Anyways, it's like it says in scripture: whosoever diggeth a pit shall fall into it. They thought they was setting a trap for me, but it was the death of them.'

The sombreness that had afflicted Joshua Morgan following the death of the two would-be bounty hunters soon passed. He didn't see that he had anything to reproach himself for: two men had pointed their weapons at him, and he had defended himself. That's how it is sometimes.

Anyway, it was difficult to remain in a sad frame of mind in the company of a boy like Tommy Walters. He was interested in everything and wanted all sorts

47

of things to be explained to him. Now that he was free of his grandfather, Tommy proved to be as merry and high-spirited a lad as one could hope to meet. Being kept a virtual prisoner had depressed his nature, but being freed of the toils, he became his old self. It made Morgan feel young again himself to hear the boy chatter and ask an unending stream of questions. Something that he did mark was that old Mister Walters had said that Tommy needed to become more manly, but Morgan had the feeling that the boy was well able to handle himself. Jacob Walters had mistaken sadness for effeminacy.

From what he recollected, Morgan believed that there was a railroad depot some fifteen or twenty miles to the west of Oakwood. This line ran all the way to St Louis, as far as he remembered, and then from there it would mean travelling through the Indian Nations to get to the Texas pan handle. He said to the boy, 'Here's the way of it. This road'll lead us to Tylerville. I don't know if we can get a train today, one as will take our horses as well, so we might have to stay there tonight.'

'Is it a big town?'

'Tolerably so. Why d'you ask?'

'Can we go and see a saloon, if there's such there?'

'No,' said Morgan definitely, 'We cannot.'

By the time they came within sight of Tylerville, the better part of three hours later, both Morgan and his young charge were ravenously hungry. Before entering the town, Morgan reined in and said, 'We need to get our story straight.'

'What story?'

'The story which explains how a roughneck like me finds himself in charge of a young child.'

'I ain't so young,' began Tommy indignantly, 'You talk like I'm a little boy.'

'This is nothing to the purpose. Truth is that a man like me, travelling with a boy your age, will excite interest and provoke questions. We need to have some explanation to offer. I'm too young to be your father, so I guess we'll have to be brothers.'

'It's wrong to tell stories, but I guess I shan't mind owning you as my brother.'

Tylersville was a bustling, modern metropolis, with every up-to-date contrivance; it even had a telegraph office. At the depot, Morgan learned what he had already more than half suspected: that they would be unable to take a train that day which would also carry their horses. One would leave tomorrow, though, at a little before midday. He paid for the necessary tickets, and then went off in search of lodgings for the horses. They found a livery stable nearby.

As they walked along the busy street, they passed the sheriff's office, where Joshua Morgan caught sight of a familiar face. On the wall outside were pasted various bills, indicating those wanted for all manner of crimes. One bore a reasonably good likeness of his own countenance, and beneath the portrait were the words 'WANTED FOR MURDER'. His own name was also emblazoned there for all to see. Upon seeing what his friend was looking at, Tommy Walters gasped and raised his arm as though he were about to point at the poster. Gently, Morgan took his hand and lowered the boy's arm, saying, 'Hush now, or we'll neither of us make it to Texas.'

After the pair of them had moved on from the sheriff's office, Tommy asked Morgan about the business, saying, 'Are you really wanted for murder? Is that why those men stopped us? The ones you. . . .'

'Do hush up, son. Yes, it's true enough that I'm wanted in connection with an event away over in Oakwood, but I never killed anybody there. I didn't so much as fire a shot.'

'So how come they say you're a murderer?'

'Here's the way of it,' said Morgan quietly, 'if you're in company with men who commit some crime and you're all part of the same outfit, then the law says you're as guilty as they are. One man fires a shot that kills someone, then all are guilty of it.'

'It don't hardly seem fair!'

'Well, that's the way of it. I'll thank you not to discuss the matter further, for if I'm taken here, then I don't know what'll become of you. Try and forget all about it.'

There was no shortage of hotels and lodging houses to be found in Tylersville, and Morgan chose a cheap and inconspicuous place near the depot. The garrulous old woman running the place was disposed to ask more questions than were comfortable, and since Morgan did not feel easy about asking a child to lie, he felt duty bound to answer all the many enquiries himself. Because he and Tommy were both famished, he was able to divert the woman into furnishing them with some victuals, which she did willingly. During the meal of chicken and dumplings, taken from vast pots simmering in her kitchen, she kept up a stream of meaningless and irrelevant observations and remarks, which nearly drove Joshua Morgan to the point of distraction. He was not himself an overly talkative man and would often rather sit quietly, rather than engage in pointless chatter.

'You come a fair distance, hey? Where you headed, out west? I don't know as I blame you. If I was a young woman, happen that's where I'd be fixing for to go. Dumplings all right, are they? That's right, they'll do you good. Got nobody else staying here right now. The two of you are welcome to set in the parlour this evening. I always like company. My, but you're both hungry. Didn't eat breakfast, hey?'

By the time the meal was ended, Morgan felt like throttling the harmless old woman and so to avoid any such precipitate action, he consented to take Tommy for a walk through the streets. It had been months since the boy had been off his grandfather's property.

As they strolled along the main street of the town, Tommy talked in an animated and excited way of seeing his mother again. 'I reckon as I'll have grown since last she saw me,' he declared, 'I hope she recognizes me straight off!'

'I make no doubt that she will,' responded Morgan, with a smile, 'A mother knows her child anywhere.'

'When did you last see your own ma, Joshua?'

'Christmas.'

'You ain't seen her for nearly a year? Why not, does she live a long way off?'

The subject was making Morgan uneasy, for he was guiltily aware that there was no earthly reason for not visiting his mother over the course of the last year. He said, 'Well, the war and all. . . .'

'That finished a long time ago.'

'Well then, let's talk of something else.'

The boy's face fell and it was clear that he was worried that he had annoyed his friend. He said, 'Are you vexed with me, sir? I mean Joshua.'

'Nohow. Let's just say that I've not been a dutiful son, leastways, not as dutiful as I might've been. There's no remedy for it presently. Maybe when I get back from seeing you safe to Texas, I'll make it up to my own ma.'

After they had strolled up and down for a spell, Morgan could not help but notice that the child was yawning. He felt guilty at seeing this, for he was suddenly aware that children should be in their beds a lot earlier than grown-up folk. It then struck him that being solely responsible for this child, the duty to put him to bed devolved upon him alone. He said, 'Time we got you safely to bed, Tommy. You've had what you might call an exciting sort of day.'

There was, a little to Morgan's surprise, no opposition to the idea of an early bedtime from the boy. Perhaps all the events of that day had been quite overwhelming for him, as he merely said, 'Just as you say, Joshua.'

A single room with two cots had seemed to Morgan the best way of arranging matters. He did not aim for the child to be out of his sight at all until he was safely delivered to his maternal parent in Texas. Experience had taught him during the war that if something *could* go wrong, then it generally *did*, sooner or later. When they reached the room, he turned his back while the boy got undressed for bed. They neither of them had night attire of any description, and so both would be obliged to sleep unclothed. When Tommy was in bed, Morgan blew out the candle, undressed and climbed into his own cot. Despite having killed two people that day, his conscience was untroubled and he fell asleep almost at once.

Joshua Morgan awoke in the pale, grey light of early dawn and for a moment could not think where he was. Then, before he opened his eyes, he was aware of a furtive rustling and stealthy movements near at hand. He gave a passable imitation of a man groaning in his sleep and then turned over, as though still securely enfolded in the arms of Morpheus. As he did this, apparently in his sleep, the furtive sounds instantly ceased. Then they resumed a few seconds after he lay still again. Morgan risked opening his eyes and saw that a man who had his back to him was searching the room as quietly and methodically as he could.

Without making any noise, Morgan pushed back the sheets and stood up. Whoever was looking through his saddle-bag was too involved in his task to notice anything amiss until Morgan was upon him and had an arm around the fellow's throat. The other man was disposed to struggle and make a fight of it, so Morgan leaned back, while keeping his arm around the man's neck, until the fellow's feet were lifted from the ground. Within a few brief seconds he felt the body grow limp as the effect of having his supply of air cut off took effect. He waited another few seconds, until he was quite sure that the man was actually unconscious, and then lowered the dead weight on to his bed. He found only one weapon, a concealed Derringer pistol, the kind of muff-gun used by gamblers and the bolder type of woman.

The brief struggle had woken Tommy, who lay in his bed with his eyes wide open, looking scared. He said, 'Is this man another of those who wants to hurt you?'

'I don't know who he is yet, son. But I aim to find out.

With the stranger's Derringer in his pocket and his own pistol cocked and aiming at the unknown man's face, Morgan felt that he was pretty much in control of the situation – but he still waited anxiously for the other to come round, so that he could be questioned. It was five minutes or so before the stranger awakened, and it was a particularly anxious wait on Joshua Morgan's part because he was worried that he had deprived the man of air for a little too long, and that perhaps the fellow would expire there in front of them. This proved not to be the case, however, and with a good deal of groaning and coughing, the man who had been searching their room regained his senses.

When Morgan was sure that he was fully conscious he spoke to him with the utmost seriousness, saying, 'I don't know who you are, but you came mighty close to losing your life. I earnestly advise you to come clean now and tell me what the game is.' The fact that throughout the course of this short speech Morgan had a Colt Army aimed directly at the face of the man to whom he was talking served to emphasize that the words he spoke were not empty threats or bluster.

In a hoarse voice, the unknown man said, 'You know me, Morgan. We was together, 'fore Bull Run. Fought at your side, what's more. My name's Will Hutton.'

A vague recollection came to Morgan's mind of sleeping in a field next to a mean fellow with a crafty face. He'd felt an instinctive aversion to the man at the time, despite the fact that he had seemed brave enough in battle. This could be the same person, he supposed. Morgan said, 'Then what? Why are you sneaking round my room in the early light of dawn this day? What's the game?'

'It's what you might call a coincidence. I saw your likeness and name on a bill outside the sheriff's office. Then, dang me if I don't see you in the flesh, strolling down the street with yon youngster. I followed you back here and waited 'til now. That's the whole of it, I swear.'

'You ain't told what you're doing in my room,' Morgan reminded him, 'Nor yet why you followed me, 'stead o' coming up to me and introducing yourself like a man.'

Will Hutton's expression was shifty and evasive, but his tail was in a crack and he was now in a spot where no amount of prevarication would serve him, so he said reluctantly, 'The poster said as you'd knocked over a bank, not all that distance from here. I guessed you'd have the proceeds of the robbery here, and so I thought I'd come and look for them. I'm down on my luck, Morgan. Ain't eaten a proper meal for weeks now.'

Morgan said, suddenly seeing the whole of the thing clearly, 'And after you'd stolen from me, you had in mind to claim the reward as well and see me hanged. That's the way of it, isn't it, you dog?'

'A man has to get by as he can.'

'I ought to kill you right now.'

Tommy Walters, who both men had forgotten was a witness to the proceedings, said in a frightened voice, 'You're not going to hurt him, are you Joshua?'

Joshua Morgan said nothing, but looked in disgust at the craven and cowardly creature in front of him. Knowing what he did now, he wished that he had choked the life out of the man in that first struggle, but he knew that he could not now set out to kill Hutton in cold blood – especially not in front of a child. He said to Tommy, 'Here's the way of it, son. If we up and leave now and do nothing with this wretch, he'll lay an information against me as soon as we're out of sight. Just for the money, you know. I can't take a chance on that. Chance, did I say? Hell, it's a sporting certainty.'

Neither Hutton nor the boy knew what this meant, whether or not Morgan was about to do murder. This was all to the good, for the longer that Will Hutton was kept in fear of his life, the less he was apt to cut up rough when Morgan revealed his actual plan. At last, he said, 'I'm going to bind you hand and foot, Hutton. Then I'm going to affix you to a bed and leave you to be found. By the time you're freed, me and the boy'll be long gone. Lord help you though, if our paths should ever cross again. I won't be so merciful next time, I'll tell you that for nothing.'

Weak with relief at having his life spared, Hutton said, 'I swear I'll never cross you again.'

With Hutton's own cooperation, Morgan tied his hands behind his back with a leather thong. Morgan's saddle-bag was packed full of useful odds and ends – one never knew when something such as an eighteen-inch strip of rawhide would come in useful. Hutton was so pleased at not being killed on the spot that he was only too keen to go along with Morgan's plans for him, no matter how inconvenient. At least he was escaping with his life, and there are worse things in this world than being hog-tied and fastened to a comfortable bed.

'I'll have to gag you, too,' said Morgan, 'You see that.'

'Sure, you go right ahead. I won't give a speck o' trouble, you'll see.'

By the time all this had been accomplished to Josh Morgan's satisfaction, it was, by his reckoning, about six. The train was leaving at seven, so they had an hour in hand to collect their horses from the livery stable and get themselves comfortably aboard. He could only hope that the mistress of the house would not be up to check on the room before the train left. There was no sound anywhere in the house, so he was hopeful that it would be at least a couple of hours before anybody looked in and found Hutton trussed up on the cot.

Before they left, Morgan said to Tommy Walters, 'Listen, you recall where the livery stable is?'

'Yes, sir. Nigh to the railroad depot.'

'Think you could find it on your own?'

''Course I could!'

'Well then, you scoot down the street now and tell them to get everything ready for me to collect the mounts in ten minutes. Think you can do that?'

The child shot a look at the helpless man on the

bed and said, 'Sure I can. You're not going to hurt him though, are you?'

'If you mean, will I kill him when you're out of the room, the answer's no. Run along now!'

After the boy had gone, Morgan turned to his helpless prisoner and said, 'It would greatly ease my mind to kill you, but I told the boy I'd not do it.'

Not seeing where this was tending, Hutton gazed up with terrified eyes as Morgan approached, his pistol in his hand. When he was within striking distance though, he did not shoot the other man, but grasped the gun by the barrel and struck Will Hutton squarely on his right temple, causing him to be rendered unconscious. It was to be hoped that he would not be in a position to try and free himself before the train left the depot in something less than an hour's time.

CHAPTER 4

The railroad train rattled and rumbled its way across the grassy plain. It was a long journey to St Louis – better than five hundred miles as the crow flew, and perhaps half as much as that again, by the time all the small diversions to avoid steep hills and deep rivers were taken into account.

Morgan had allowed the boy to have the seat by the window and he sat there, his eyes shining, as he watched the miles being eaten up by the thundering locomotive that drew the coaches and vans across Ohio. Joshua Morgan was sunk in his own thoughts. Even if Hutton had freed himself, or been freed by somebody else, even a minute or so after their train had left Tylersville, there wasn't one chance in a thousand that anything would come of it to cause Morgan and his young friend any difficulty. In the first place, it was to be doubted that anybody would be minded to pay Hutton for the information that the wanted bank robber Joshua Morgan had lately

60

been in the town, but his whereabouts were currently unknown. The law was notoriously unwilling to part with reward money, even under ideal circumstances where the man had been actually apprehended and handed over to them. Nobody was going to give Hutton a cent for claiming that he had just seen and spoken to a wanted man, but had no notion of where he was now.

Then again, Morgan hoped that he might have put the fear of God into the weasel, and that Will Hutton would more likely slink off into the shadows than risk encountering Morgan again one day. No, from all that he could see, there was little chance of pursuit from the lawmen of Tylersville. Which meant that, taking various stops into account for the purposes of taking on water and allowing passengers to relieve themselves at intervals, another twenty-four hours or so should see them fetching up in St Louis – from which city they should be able to get another train to Springfield, Missouri.

This was where the whole scheme was a little hazy in Morgan's eyes, for they would need to cross the Indian Nations if the idea was to get to Texas as soon as might be. It was no doubt possible to travel by rail north and west, then entering the Texas Panhandle from the west – but as far as Joshua Morgan was concerned, the sooner this child was delivered back to his mother, the better. A longer journey meant more hazard and uncertainty, and he just wished to do this job as quickly and neatly as he was able.

Sitting opposite Morgan and the boy were an elderly and respectable-looking couple, and it was obvious that they were consumed with curiosity about the strangely mismatched pair facing them. After lying to the woman running the lodging house, Morgan did not feel inclined to encourage Tommy to tell anybody else that they were brothers, and so had related on the train a modified version of the truth, saying that he was the child's tutor. But he was powerful young though for such a responsible position, and hardly gave the impression of being an educated man. The man and woman therefore watched the two of them narrowly, not satisfied with the story that they had been told, but not sure either if there was something illegal or immoral about this rough-looking young man accompanying a young boy on such a long journey.

Morgan and the boy dozed fitfully on the train and then spent the night in a hotel in St Louis, catching the next train needed, the one to Springfield, early the following morning. This was all fairly gruelling, and Morgan asked himself at times if he wasn't setting the pace a little too harshly for so young a child. There was, however, a sense of urgency about the whole enterprise, because the longer the two of them were on the road, the more the odds shortened on some busybody in an official capacity taking an interest in them. The old couple on the train to St Louis had been annoying, but nothing worse. Imagine though, thought Morgan to himself, if he and Tommy found themselves sitting opposite a lawman or something of that kind.

Morgan's anxiety about the speed at which he was making them travel was by no means shared by his young companion. After being trapped in his grandfather's house for months, Tommy Walters was having a whale of a time, seeing a never-ending stream of new places and undergoing novel experiences every day. Travelling hundreds of mile by train, staying first in a lodging house and then a hotel, riding on horseback for a long way, seeing men being shot and killed: it was all as good as a dime novel or magic lantern show! Although he longed to see his mother again, he could not help but find the whole journey a constant delight. After they had spent a night in the hotel in St Louis, another first for the boy, he said to Morgan, 'Are we really going to ride through Indian country?'

'We're going to cross the Indian Nations, for sure. But it's quiet enough there just now, and I don't look for any trouble.'

It was not until the train drew into Springfield that the reality of the situation really dawned on Tommy and he began to feel a mite uneasy about it all. As they left the depot, he said nervously, 'Joshua, are you sure those Indians aren't on the warpath?'

Morgan laughed and took the liberty of ruffling the boy's hair affectionately. 'Nothing of the kind,' he said, 'It'll be like a hunting trip. You ever slept out of doors before? Under the stars?'

'No, sir.'

'Well then, now's your chance.'

'Won't we freeze? It's coming on winter.'

Morgan chuckled again. 'We won't freeze, not this far south, not at this time o' year. 'Sides, we'll be lighting ourselves a fire. Every boy should get a chance for this sort of trip. Better than a heap of book-learning! We'll have some rare fun.'

Although sitting opposite the inquisitive old couple on the train to St Louis had made Morgan a little uneasy, he had more or less forgotten about this when he and Tommy walked down the street from Springfield's railroad depot that afternoon, having lodged their horses in a nearby livery stable. But he was reminded of his earlier misgivings when a strong-looking fellow with a pewter badge on his coat stopped them and remarked in a friendly enough fashion, 'You two seem an ill-matched pair. Mind telling me who you are and where you're headed?' Looking at the dull grey star on the fellow's lapels, Morgan realized that matters might be about to get a little complicated, for the star bore the single word inscription, 'Sheriff'.

'It's by way of being a long story...' began Morgan, but it appeared that the sheriff was not minded to listen to some hasty explanation on the sidewalk.

'I'll be bound it is,' he said amiably. 'Tell you what, why don't the both of you come down a-ways to my office? You don't want to be chatting your business to the whole world, I'm sure.'

Although he spoke in a friendly enough manner to them, Morgan noticed that the sheriff stood off far enough that he would have time to draw his piece if Morgan showed any inclination to get rough. As he directed them towards his office, the fellow also took care to be walking a little behind them, so that he was not apt to be taken by surprise from behind. Here was a man who spoke softly, but surely knew his business. This was abundantly confirmed in Morgan's eyes when the sheriff's hand suddenly snaked forward and removed Morgan's pistol from the holster, before he had a chance even to turn around.

The sheriff's office was empty, and when he had ushered Josh Morgan and his young friend through the door ahead of him, he indicated two chairs and said affably, 'Make yourselves comfortable.' When the two of them were seated, he continued, 'I'll warrant the two of you came here from the general direction of St Louis, am I right?' While posing this question, he kept his eyes fixed on Tommy, who at once glanced at Morgan to see how he was supposed to answer this enquiry. Noticing this, the sheriff said, 'Ah, you're not sure how much you can say in the presence of this man, is that the way of it? Don't fret, I'm going to make that right.'

As far as Morgan could make out, it was all up with him. This lawman was minded to play games before arresting him, but if he knew that they had come from St Louis, then odds were that he was conversant with the rest of the story. Pretty soon, he would be locked up and then transported back to the scene of the failed bank robbery to stand trial for murder. Having resigned himself mentally to this melancholy sequence of events, he was puzzled when the sheriff began explaining further why he had brought them in. As the story unfolded, a faint spark of hope began glowing in Morgan's heart: maybe matters were not quite so desperate as he had assumed.

'Truth is, I been waiting for you two. Well, not the two of you personally, you know, but two like you. You got to know, I'm on top of what's going on, and I mean to make life hot for those running that orphans' asylum.'

Mention of an orphans' asylum puzzled Morgan exceedingly and gave him cause to hope that this was a case of mistaken identity, and that he and Tommy might yet be freed. He said, 'I don't rightly understand you.'

'Do you not? Well then, I'm guessing that this young fellow thinks that you're taking him to a nice home, where he'll be loved and cared for and treated with every kindness. Ain't that so, young'un?' he turned to Tommy and watched his reaction to this statement. Because he was indeed heading home to his mother, the boy could hardly dispute the sheriff's assessment that he was being taken somewhere he'd be loved and treated with kindness. He shrugged, not knowing what was going on.

'What it is, you see, is that I know all about this

game. How the folk at the orphans' asylum tell you boys that you're going somewhere where you'll be treated like real sons, but how in fact you fetch up on farms where you have to work damned hard and get little enough food and sleep. I know you won't tell me the truth with this fellow near at hand, but I'm fixing for to lock him up in back here and take you off to stay with a minister's family. You can tell them all about it, and I promise no harm'll befall you.'

During this little speech by the sheriff, the scales had fallen from Joshua Morgan's eyes and he saw what all this talk about orphans was connected with. Indeed, he had heard of this business before, although not in this part of the country. Some orphanages more or less sold off strong and able boys as farm labourers or apprentices. It saved them the cost of feeding them, and also brought in money from those prepared to pay a lump sum for a worker who would not require wages for a few years. The death of so many breadwinners during the late war had greatly increased the number of children who were either orphans or whose families could not afford to feed and clothe them.

It seemed to Morgan that there was now a good chance that he could clear up this misunderstanding, and that he and Tommy could be on their way to spend a night in a hotel. He said, 'Listen, I know now of what you speak. I see why you want to put a stop to this trade. It's almost like slavery under another name. But me and the boy here, we're nothing to do with such goings on. Why don't you ask him?'

'Why, that's just what I aim to do. But not with you around. I'm affeared as he wouldn't speak freely in your presence. But if it's all as you say, and you ain't just fetched him from that orphans' asylum just down the line to St Louis, why then you and he can be on your way tomorrow, free as the wind.' The look on the sheriff's face suggested that he did not think this a likely outcome, for he continued, 'Mind, I'll have to send a few wires, check up on whatever story you tell me.'

It was at this point that Morgan realized that he was almost certain to be revealed soon as the missing member of the Anderson Gang, wanted for robbery and murder. Tommy would surely tell the story of how he had been living at his grandfather's home, and once that was checked, then it was a fair bet that any lawman worth his salt would ask himself who this young man was that he was travelling with. As soon as the town of Oakwood was mentioned, somebody would start thinking about any possible connection between a young man fleeing west and the wanted fugitive, Joshua Morgan.

On the desk that lay between him and the sheriff, Morgan observed a heavy glass vase, which contained a spray of dried grasses. It was an oddly feminine touch in such a place. He calculated that by the size and thickness of it, the vase must weigh at least a pound or more. The sheriff stood up and said, 'Well, my friend, I'm hopeful that you'll consent to enter

the cell at back of this office without any unpleasant-
ness?'

'Just as you say,' responded Morgan, a hangdog
and defeated expression on his face. He rose from
the seat and then, with astonishing swiftness,
snatched up the heavy vase and hurled it full at the
sheriff's face. It caught the man squarely on the fore-
head and he staggered back, clutching one hand to
his face and fumbling for his pistol with the other.
Already, though, Morgan was moving round the
desk. His own confiscated pistol had been set down
carelessly on the desk, so sure had this fellow been
that he was not dealing with anybody likely to prove
a real danger. Well, thought Morgan as he grabbed it
by the barrel, that just goes to show how wrong you
can be about folk.

The sheriff was still dazed and he had only just
managed to get his own pistol free of the holster,
when Josh Morgan began viciously pistol-whipping
him about the head and face, until the man slumped
to the floor, unconscious. He wondered if he had
actually killed him, but there was no time to fret
about such a possibility now. Morgan had already
noted the metal hoop hanging on the wall, from
which hung a variety of large keys. Guessing that one
of these would be for the cell of which he had been
told, Morgan reached up and took the keys from the
wall. Then he dragged the body towards the back of
the office. He was relieved to note that the man was
breathing, although shallowly and rapidly, as though

he were in shock. At least he was still alive, and that was something.

Tommy Walters remained in his chair, his only reaction so far being a widening of his eyes as he watched the savage assault on the peaceful and quiet-talking lawman. Morgan considered asking the boy to lend a hand with dragging the unconscious sheriff to the cell, but thought better of it. Why should he involve an innocent child in this kind of action? Just as he had supposed, one of the keys on the metal hoop fitted the gate to a barred enclosure, little larger than a broom closet, and it was here that Morgan dumped his burden, locking the door behind him. Then he returned to the main part of the office and told the scared-looking boy, 'We need to ride for the Territories right this very minute.'

'I thought we was going to a hotel?'

'Not any more. We're fetching our horses and leaving. Now.' As the boy remained sitting there and showed no sign of shifting, Morgan said forcefully, 'This is a hanging matter. We don't get away at once, I'm goin' to get my neck stretched.'

Even as the two of them walked briskly to the livery stable where they had left their horses just a half hour earlier, Morgan was uncomfortably aware that he had committed a brutal assault on what seemed like decent fellow, purely in order to save his own skin. Worse, he had embroiled an innocent child in the affair. This had not been to rescue Tommy Walters, but solely because he was in fear for his own life. Doubtless the sheriff would have soon found out the story from young Tommy, and been better placed to reunite him with his mother safely and expeditiously than Morgan was. No, dress it up how you liked, the attack he had just made, which could easily have ended in murder, had been carried out only for his own sake. There was nothing noble about it, and he hadn't even been thinking of Tommy when he lamped that sheriff.

It was possible that something along the same lines was now going through Tommy's head, for when he glanced sideways at the boy, there was a very serious and thoughtful expression on his young face. True, he had just witnessed a shocking act of violence, but he had recovered fast enough from seeing Morgan kill two men. The boy was, by the look of him, doing some serious thinking. Perhaps he was wondering if he had taken a wrong turn by agreeing to ride alongside Joshua Morgan. Well, he wouldn't be the first who had had such misgivings, and that was a fact. At the thought, and despite the desperate circumstances, Morgan smiled.

Although puzzled and not a little annoyed at having to bring their mounts out after such a short while, the owner of the livery stable knew that he was making money for very little work on his part. It took Morgan just a few minutes to tack up his horse and Tommy's pony, and then they were off, heading west towards the Indian Nations.

A word or two might not come amiss at this point

about the Indian Nations, or the 'Territories' as they were sometimes known. As the settlers pushed ever further west during the first half of the nineteenth century, they inevitably came into conflict with the tribes whose lands they were intent upon stealing. It was hardly surprising that this led to what some have called the 'Indian wars'. Treaties were made and then broken with such monotonous regularity that it is little wonder that the 'red' men came to distrust and treat with the gravest suspicion, anything told them by the white men.

Gradually the Indians were squeezed into smaller and smaller geographical areas, ranging from the so-called 'reservations', all the way up to a stretch of land that was larger than most states. This was the home of what were known as the 'five civilized tribes', namely the Cherokee, Chickasaw, Choctaw, Creek and Seminole. This area, which was later to become the state of Oklahoma, was guaranteed to the Indians in perpetuity, and was called the Indian Territories or Indian Nations.

Needless to say, the treaties and guarantees that established the Indian Nations were worth no more than all the previous treaties, and after the end of the War between the States an excuse was sought to dispossess the Indians of these lands too, and open them up to white settlers. The justification that was settled on was that the Indians had supported the Confederacy during the late war, and in so doing had forfeited their right to possible statehood. At the time when Josh Morgan and Tommy Walters were setting off to cross the Territories, they were by way of being a debateable land, which was in theory governed by the inhabitants, with no reference to the rest of the nation.

This peculiar state of affairs made the Territories an ideal place for runaways, fugitives from justice, outlaws and all manner of other folk who, for various reasons, wished to live in a place where the normal law of the land did not apply. Taking a child across such country was not a move that anybody other than a man desperately fleeing from the shadow of the noose would have countenanced for a moment.

There was no sound of a hue and cry being raised as Morgan and his young companion trotted their horses down Springfield's main street, towards the edge of town. With luck, it would be a few hours before anybody would notice that their sheriff was missing. What would happen then was anybody's guess. Would the man feel aggrieved enough to raise a posse and come after them? Morgan had known stranger things to happen. Almost as though Tommy had read his mind, he asked while Morgan was mulling these matters over, 'Do you think that anybody will chase us? Because of the sheriff, I mean.'

'I wouldn't have thought so,' said Morgan thoughtfully, 'Although you never can tell. There was one time. . . .' Then he recollected himself, and realized that the story of how he evaded capture after robbing a railroad train was not precisely a suitable one for telling to a boy of ten. Instead he said, 'Anyways, I think we should be all right.'

'Why did you hit that man? He seemed kind.'

Morgan did not reply to this innocent inquiry for fully a minute, and finally said, 'A man's life is what matters to him most of all, when you come right down to it. If I'd o' let him lock me up in that cell and start asking about where I'd been and who I was, then sure as God made little green apples, it would end by me being taken back to Oakwood and hanged.'

'Couldn't you've explained to him?'

'Not hardly,' replied Morgan, a twisted grin on his face, 'I never yet seed a lawman as would turn a blind eye to a murderer or bank robber he thought he'd apprehended. It's not in reason that any would do such.'

'I bet he would've seen I got home safely, though.'

There was nothing to be said to this, because it was undeniably true. For the sake of his own skin, Morgan had carried out a murderous attack in front of a child and was now taking that same child into some of the wildest and most lawless stretches of country in the whole of the United States. He might have embarked upon this quest with the best intentions in the world, but he was hardly a fit and proper guardian for a child. It was strange, but he had never been one for feeling guilty or ashamed, but now the sense of shame rose within him, and he found to his dismay that he was blushing like a girl. He turned his face to one side, hoping that Tommy would not see that he had gone red.

At first when they left town, they passed through an area of fields and cultivated land. Then the settlements grew sparser and stopped. Within a half hour, the two of them were in wild and untamed country. Morgan tried to keep up a fairly brisk pace, by trotting for a while and then getting the boy to canter along of him, until he had had enough. For all that he had said that Springfield's sheriff would not be coming after them, he did not really know the score.

There was nothing to indicate when the two of them left the state of Missouri and entered the Indian Nations. Theoretically, Morgan was now free from the hazard of pursuit by an enraged man who had received a few hefty blows to his head and seen his authority set at naught, but he was only too well aware that whatever the legal niceties, lawmen could, and did, chase men into the Territories, capture them and then take them off to stand trial elsewhere. He would just have to take great care that such a fate did not befall him.

'Is this all Indian country?' asked Tommy. 'Do any white folk live here at all?'

'Well, they ain't supposed to, but you know how it is. Some come to live here because they're wanted men. Others think they can make a living here easier than they can in more civilized parts.'

'You ever been here before?'

'During the war. Fought a battle here.'

'What was it like?'

'Fighting in a war? Just terrible. Like nothing you've ever seen, even in the worst nightmare you ever had.'

That night they slept in the open. Because they had lit out of Springfield in such a hurry, there had been no opportunity to buy food, but Morgan had the remains of a loaf of bread and a little cheese. This they toasted over the fire he built, washing it down with copious draughts of ice-cold water from a nearby stream. The weather was clement, and it did not look as though they were likely to freeze to death, notwithstanding Tommy's earlier fears. As they sat there, peering into the flames of their little fire, Tommy said, 'I'm grateful really for being with you. I was just scared before.'

'You'd good cause to be so,' replied the other gloomily. 'I can't think what your grandpapa was about, entrusting your very life to a wretch like me. Well, there it is, there's naught to be done now to remedy the situation. Still and all, it was badly done. I can scarcely take care of my own self, never mind look after a child.'

When they lay down to sleep that night, the boy taking the blanket and Morgan making shift as best he could, Tommy fell asleep almost immediately, as children sometimes do after an especially exciting or tiring day. As for Morgan, he lay awake for the better part of two hours, fathoming matters out in his mind.

He knew that he had done a wrong and selfish thing by bringing the boy into this wild country, and he felt ashamed of himself for putting his own interests first in this way.

It wouldn't do, and he knew that he would never be able to live with himself if he exposed the child to hazard by getting him to travel two hundred miles across Indian country like this, a stretch of land infested with bandits, savages and who knew what all else. There was nothing for it, he would have to return him to Springfield and leave the proper authorities to make the necessary arrangements. He only hoped that he could escape with his own neck intact after taking such a step. It was then, for the first time since he was himself a child, that Joshua Morgan found himself invoking the aid of the deity. He had not been a one for prayer, even during the most ferocious fighting of the war, but now he muttered softly: 'Lord, only bring that child to safety and let me keep my own life, and I promise I'm going to change. I can't continue so.' This felt strangely satisfying, and when he drifted off to sleep, Morgan was at peace with the world for the first time in a good long while.

CHAPTER 5

When he woke up the next morning, Morgan felt a sudden surge of sheer pleasure, the joy that comes when a man knows that he is doing the right thing, however irksome it might be. Then he opened his eyes and saw that Tommy was not at his side. The blanket was there, but the boy was not. He was not at first unduly alarmed, assuming that the boy had simply wandered off to answer a call of nature. Then he looked uneasily around the little grove of trees among which they had camped. There was a clear and unobstructed view of the open grassland beyond the ring of trees, and there was no sign of movement anywhere.

Morgan sat up and shouted at the top of his voice, 'Tommy! Where are you, boy?' A flock of birds that had been pecking the ground nearby, took fright and flew up into the sky with a clatter of wings – but there was no reply to his calling.

Seriously alarmed now, Morgan leaped to his feet and went in search of his young charge. It took but a few minutes to establish for certain sure what he had already known in his heart was the case: Tommy Walters had vanished.

When he was perfectly assured that the child was nowhere in the vicinity, and was not hiding near at hand as some kind of practical joke, Morgan returned to the campsite and sat down to reason the matter through. As far as he could see, there were only two possibilities: either Tommy had wandered off or run away by his own volition, or he had been abducted against his will. The former being improbable in the extreme, it seemed to Morgan that the boy must have been carried away by some person or persons unknown, which was a chilling thought. It went only to confirm what an inadequate guardian he had been in the first place. He'd no business to have been bringing the child here. Reproaching himself, though, would not bring Tommy back. He racked his brains to think of what his next move ought to be, seeing as he hadn't the faintest idea even in which direction the boy had been taken.

When he had passed through the Territories a year or so back, in the closing stages of the war, Morgan recalled that there had been a little trading post near to where he was currently situated. It was run by a dour and uncommunicative white man who had a squaw wife. As Morgan recollected, the trading post had been combined with a little *cantina*, in the Mexican style, little more than a makeshift lean-to against the side of the house in which the man lived. Now, what was his name?

After a little more thought, Morgan came up with the name of Abbot. Was his Christian name Joe? At any rate, the drinking place that he owned had been, by popular account, a meeting place for all manner of rootless drifters, deserters, spies, outcasts and men without pasts. Having no other ideas on how to recover Tommy, heading to Abbot's place seemed about the only way to proceed that Morgan could come up with.

In theory, the whole of the Indian Territories belonged absolutely to the members of the five civilized tribes, and no white man could settle there without their express permission and consent. This may well have been the legal situation, but it was a point of law honoured more in the breach than the observance. There was plenty of room for everybody in the Territories, and if white men wished to take their chances there on an informal and wholly illegal basis, then nobody stopped them from doing so.

Abbot had proved a useful addition to the district in which he dwelt, supplying the local inhabitants with cheap pots and pans, mirrors, beads and even firearms, receiving in return pelts and furs, odd nuggets of gold and even cash money. But the little eating place and watering hole that he ran was strictly for white folk. He drew the line at supplying Indians with strong drink, having seen in the past what a terrible thing it was when a bunch of young braves got liquored up.

When he arrived at the high ridge of land overlooking Abbot's place, Morgan reined in his horse and caused Tommy's pony, which he was leading, to halt too. It was just as he remembered it. A stout, stone-built house with a ramshackle wooden structure leaning against it. The trading part of the enterprise took place at front of the house, and the *cantina* was at the back. Whether he really would hear tidings of the whereabouts of Tommy Walters here, he could not say, but for want of any better scheme, Morgan thought that he might at least try.

The *cantina* at the back of Joe Abbot's house was hardly larger than an average-sized room. The walls were made of roughly hewn planks that were fitted together without any caulking. A natural consequence was that the place was very draughty and sometimes wet, when the wind blew driving rain through the gaps. The seating consisted of sections of sawn tree trunks, which doubled as both chairs and also supports for the tables, which were just planks nailed across other and larger pieces of tree.

Although it was early morning, Morgan was surprised to find that a half-dozen men were lounging around. A few were eating and the others simply sitting and smoking. He assumed that they must have been sleeping nearby, and had come here now to break their fast. Behind a rough table, upon which was set a steaming Dutch pot, stood the proprietor of the establishment. Morgan decided to approach matters circuitously and so began by smiling broadly and saying, 'Hi there! I was here before. During the war, you know.'

Abbot was notorious for his brusque and unfriendly demeanour. He replied, 'Truth to tell, stranger, I ain't a one for talking over old times over-much. You want to eat?'

'Well, I was hoping to talk a little, if you've time.'

'You want to talk, I suggest you join a debating society or such. I serve food and liquor here. You planning on eating or leaving?'

'Well, now you mention it, I could do with some vittles. Could you let me have some bread, butter and cheese?'

Joe Abbot regarded Morgan with considerable disfavour and said, 'Listen, I don't know where you hail from, but happen you're mixing this place up with some fancy hotel, like they have in the east. We don't run to what you might call an extensive menu. This here Dutchie has pork and beans in it. You want some or not?'

'I will, thank you. I've not eaten much for the last day or so.'

While Abbot was filling a grimy bowl with the comestibles, an Indian woman whom Morgan took to be his wife appeared, and began sweeping the dirt floor of the place in a desultory fashion with a besom. Having paid for the food, Morgan said, 'Fact is, I'm looking for a little boy. I was travelling with him and he's gone missing. I was wondering if anybody here could shed light on the business?' He turned to include those seated at the tables in his inquiry. 'Has anybody seen a child of ten hereabouts? He was sleeping at my side last night, and now he's gone.'

Morgan might have been speaking Greek for all the reaction he gained. After gazing at him curiously, the six men turned back to eating and talking. Abbot leaned forward and said quietly, 'A word of advice, mister. People round here don't take kindly to folk asking questions, you hear what I tell you? Includes me, case you was wondering.'

'This is a child I'm talking of. Little boy of just ten years of age. I'm hoping to get him safely home to his ma. I'm not looking to create trouble, and I don't give a tinker's cuss what any of these boys are about. I just want a lead on where to find that youngster.'

While he was speaking, the squaw had come up and gripped Abbot's arm. She was talking rapidly in some unknown language and gesticulating with her free hand. Abbot was shaking his head doggedly, but the woman was not giving up on whatever she was trying to get across. At length, Abbot said, 'Maybe you would favour me with a word in private.' Wondering what was going on, Morgan followed the man and woman outside, where Abbot continued,

'My wife here would have me tell you something. There's a band of Choctaw, not far from here. They don't settle, just roam around like in the old days. Those folk sometimes snatch children, use 'em as servants and suchlike. I say "servants", slaves is what I mean. Mostly Indian children, those from other tribes, but I've heard o' white children being took, too.'

Having delivered himself of what was, for him, a speech comparable in length to the Gettysberg address, Joe Abbot turned to leave, shooing his wife forward as he did so. Morgan's lip curled and he said contemptuously, 'You knew all that, and it took a woman to make you speak out? Nice fellow you are, and I don't think!'

The master of the house ignored this insult and went back inside. Morgan followed and fell to devouring his food, for he found now that he was ravenously hungry. None of the other men present spoke to Morgan or even looked in his direction, which suited him well enough. He guessed that it would be pointless to ask if anybody had any information on the whereabouts of the Choctaw who were apparently in the area. Well, he had tracked men before and would just have to do so again. It was the devil of a business. Just when he had decided to do the right thing and return the child to Springfield, this had to happen. How he was going to rescue the boy from a band of Indians, even if he should find them, was more than Morgan knew. One thing he *did* know for certain, though, was that unless he did, he would never sleep easy again, nor be able to face himself in the mirror while shaving. It was he who had set the child at hazard while attempting to save his own wretched skin, and it was up to him now to remedy the situation or die in the attempt.

After returning the empty bowl to Abbot, who was standing gloomily by his pot, Morgan left the place without another word. He was getting ready to mount up when one of the customers came out and walked up to him, saying, 'I think you and me are destined to ride side by side for a spell, friend.'

Morgan looked the other man over with frank distaste. In front of him stood a fellow of perhaps forty-five or fifty years of age. He looked like an outdoors kind of a person, for his face was leathery and weather-beaten. The long, grey, greasy-looking hair was drawn back into something resembling a horse's tail. Morgan's guess would have been trapper or mountain man, had it not been for the look of sly and crafty intelligence in the man's eyes. Looking into those eyes made Morgan feel unaccountably uneasy, and it was his considered opinion that this was one of the most unprepossessing individuals who had crossed his path in a good long while. For this reason, his first impulse when the man suggested that they were about to ride together was to growl something along the lines of, 'Not while I got breath in my body!' – but he managed to restrain himself, and said instead, 'I don't rightly understand what you mean. Far as I can tell, we never even met.'

A cunning look flickered momentarily in the man's eyes, as though he were fencing with Morgan or playing some game. He said, 'Well, truth is, we're both looking for a boy who's a little shy of his eleventh birthday. Coincidence, don't you think?'

Morgan shrugged indifferently. 'Couldn't say, I'm sure.'

'Let's lay down our cards and see what we got. I'm a-searching, among other things, for a boy called Tom Walters. That who you're after as well?'

'What's your interest in the matter?'

'So you are! It's just as I say, we can work together.'

'I don't think it for a moment,' said Morgan firmly, 'Not until I know a good deal more about you than I do now. Who are you?'

'My name's Judd. I find folk – if it's worth my while, that is to say. I guess you know there's a reward been offered for to track down that Tom Walters and take him home? If he's still alive, that is, which didn't seem likely to me, until you fetched up here.'

For a few seconds, Joshua Morgan thought this over. Then he said, 'First off is, I didn't know anything about a reward. The boy's alive, at least he was last night. What do you mean when you say you find folk "if it's worth your while"?'

'Oh, you know,' said Judd easily, 'Folk as other folk are looking for.'

'No, I don't know. What d'you mean?'

The other man shrugged, not in the least affronted by Morgan's tone, which was anything but agreeable. 'Say a man's run away from the law. . . .'

Before the sentence had been completed, Morgan grimaced and looked at the other with disgust. 'You're a bounty man. I might o' guessed.'

'Then what? You want to get this child, and so do I. If he's really been taken by a bunch of Choctaw, two can free him better than one man working alone.'

'How'd you know about this? Me and Abbot were talking quiet outside.'

'The squaw was shooting her mouth off earlier inside. Lucky I understand a bit o' Cherokee.'

There was, without the shadow of a doubt, some sense in what this unpleasant-looking fellow said. Two would definitely have a better chance of freeing Tommy than one alone. Not only that, but Morgan had a hunch that this might be somebody who would be able to find the Choctaw, which he was by no means sure that he would be able to do alone. While he was musing in this way, Judd said, 'Only thing is, you must take oath that you ain't after any of that reward money. We get the boy, that's all mine.'

'That's all in order,' said Morgan, adding, 'But I'll tell you this, and you best listen well. If I find you're not as you represent, and that you cause any harm to that little boy, I give you my word, I'll kill you.'

'That mean it's a deal?'

Much as he loathed the idea of working next to a

bounty hunter, Morgan could see that this turn of events might actually work out for the best. He said, 'I guess so. You have any notion where these blessed Choctaw are to be found?'

Judd's face split in a broad smile. 'Yes, I should just about say that I do.'

As the two men rode away from Abbot's place in the direction confidently indicated by the man who called himself Judd, Josh Morgan tried to rationalize his longstanding aversion to those who chose the calling of bounty hunters. Like most men who lived on the wrong side of the law, Morgan had never had any particular hatred or even dislike of lawmen. He knew fine well that there had to be laws, and it followed that some men had to be employed in making sure that folk obeyed those laws. That was all very right and proper. He had no grievance against such men, who for the most part seemed genuinely to care about the maintenance of order and protecting the weak against the ruthless and strong. The bounty hunter, though, was something else again.

When a reward was posted for a wanted man, anybody could collect the money if they brought in the criminal. Sometimes there were conditions attached to the reward, that the prisoner must be brought back alive, say, or that the money was payable only on conviction in a properly constituted court of law. Mostly, though, nobody much cared if the felon was killed when being apprehended.

Judd, divining the meaning of Morgan's reluctance to talk to him, said amiably, 'I guess you don't care for men like me, hey?'

'Since you ask, no. Not overmuch.'

Not at all put out, the bounty man continued jovially, 'Well, a lot of folk feel the same. What a mercy that I ain't a sensitive type of fellow, or I'd be all broke up by now.'

Trying to change the subject, Morgan asked, 'How far we likely to be travelling this day?'

'Depends where them Indians are.'

'Thought you knew?'

'Said I'd a notion, but we still need to look for 'em.'

The two men did not speak for the next half hour or so, which suited Morgan just fine. Tommy's pony seemed content to trail along on the end of a rope, and there was little for Morgan to do but wonder if this Judd really knew anything about the location of the Choctaw, and if this whole expedition was no more than a snipe hunt. Suddenly Judd reined in and leaped down from his mount. He fell to the ground and stared hard at some marks that he could seemingly make out in the scrubby grass. For his part, Morgan could discern nothing of any significance – but then again, he had never really been either a tracker or scout.

After a minute or two of watching the man sniffing around on the ground like a bloodhound, Morgan said impatiently, 'Well, you see anything?'

'Yeah,' said Judd, standing up, 'I reckon a horse passed this way in the night, carrying some kind of heavy burden. Could be what we're after.'

'You best not be fooling with me you know,' said Morgan, 'You can really see that, from just looking at the grass and mud?'

'You want to take over and find these boys for your own self?'

Morgan shook his head.

'Then let me do the tracking. Dare say you have some skill with a gun, but I reckon you'd be lost now were it not for me.'

It took until midday before they caught up with the band for whom they were seeking. About three miles away, across a broad and shallow valley, they could just about discern a mass of people, although at that distance it was impossible to pick out individuals. They looked like ants crawling across a floor.

'You think that's them?' asked Morgan, 'I could surely do with a pair of field-glasses.'

'That's the ones we're after. But now that the hare is in sight, as you might say, I'll own that I ain't been exactly straight with you.'

'How's that?' said Morgan, fixing the other with a cold eye, 'You best not have misled me about that child, I'll tell you that for nothing.'

'Fact is, I wasn't looking for this Tommy Walters when you fetched up at Abbot's place. Knew about him going missing, of course, and the reward and all. Truth to tell, I thought the same as most everybody else, that he was dead. Mind, I kept it in the back of my mind. After all, two hundred dollars is always worth having. It's what you might term a happy coincidence. I was trailing those Choctaws for quite another reason.'

'Meaning that when you heard me talking about the boy I was looking for, and what Abbot's wife said, you worked out what had happened to Tommy and thought you'd found a chance to cash in?'

'You got that right, boy!'

Joshua Morgan sat silently, struggling to maintain his equanimity. If the man at his side knew how close he was to being shot down like a dog, he gave no sign of it, merely reaching into his jacket, fishing out a tobacco pouch and rolling himself a cigarette while Morgan digested what he had just been told. When he had brought his emotions under control, Morgan said in a tight voice, 'Would you care to say why you were after those Indians in the first place?'

'That's no mystery. There's a brave riding with 'em as is wanted for some beastliness in Texas. He and some others raided a lonely farm. Killed most everybody, raped the women first, you know how it goes. But there was one girl left alive, they never knew she was there. She described him, and he's what you might call of a distinctive appearance. There's a tidy sum to be made by bringing him back. Best of it is that it's the same price dead or alive.'

'You expect me to aid you in this filthy business of bounty hunting?'

'You will if this boy is so precious to you, yes,' replied Judd, not in the least abashed, 'I can't tell you what a godsend you are to me.'

It was at this point, when he realized that this loathsome specimen had played him for a fool, just for what he saw as Tommy's monetary value, that Morgan swore to himself that he would make sure that Judd did not benefit in any way from the child's recovery. For his own part, he wanted no reward: it was his bounden duty to fetch that child and see him safely home. It was his own folly that had brought the boy to this pass, and the very least he could do was to set matters right. But the slinking cur smoking peacefully beside him would not make a single cent out of the thing, of that Morgan was well assured. Not allowing any of this to show in his face or demeanour, he said mildly, 'How do you say we should proceed? Bearing in mind, too, that we don't know for sure yet that Tommy is even there with them?'

Relieved that his dupe had taken this so well, Judd said, 'No point starting a war with 'em. We'll wait 'til nightfall when they camp. They won't be expecting anybody to walk right in, I shouldn't think.'

So large was the territory set aside at that time for the five tribes to live in, encompassing as it did the whole of what was one day to become the state of Oklahoma and more, that there was plenty of room for those who wished to pursue their traditional, nomadic lifestyle. True, some of the Indians settled down and built homes, tilling the earth as farmers. This was, by and large, what the government in Washington desired. They earnestly hoped that the formerly bloodthirsty wanderers of the plains would become pastoralists, and in time indistinguishable from their white neighbours.

However, not all the men in the Territories wanted to adopt an agrarian way of life. The Choctaw especially continued to roam from place to place, hunting game and sometimes looting from their more peaceful and settled neighbours. But the days of such activities were now strictly numbered, and some, in desperation, were talking of launching a final war against the white men. There could hardly be a worse time for two white men to try and sneak into the camp of such folk and try and steal away not only one of their slaves, but also a warrior at the peak of his vitality and strength.

'When do you think they'll stop for the night?' asked Morgan.

'Hour or two before dusk. Give 'em time to set up their tepees and so on.'

'They only stay one night in each camp?'

'Depends. Could be a night, might be a week or a month. The better the pickings, the longer they're apt to stick around.'

Morgan said, 'Something we need to get straight right now, Judd. You make your living like this, taking mad chances for high stakes. You're a gambler. I ain't.'

'What are you telling me, that's you've no stomach for taking risks?'

'Nobody as knew me during the late war would dare say such a thing. But I value my life, and getting that boy back to his ma is more to me than my own life. So don't try and arrange things so that I am killed and provide the distraction you need to carry out your own schemes. It won't answer.'

There was a gleam of respect in the bounty hunter's eyes, which revealed to Morgan that his guess had been close to the mark. Judd eyed him with new respect and said, 'What is it with you and that boy, anyways? Was it you that snatched him away?'

'No, it weren't.'

'I thought maybe you're one of those as prefers little boys to grown women. Not that it matters to me where a man finds his pleasure, you understand.'

Josh Morgan urged his mare forwards until it was brushing flanks with Judd's own horse and he was perhaps four feet from the other man. Whereupon he drew his pistol, cocking it with his thumb as he did so, and offered the muzzle to the other man, saying as he did so, 'Say that once more. . . .'

Already repenting of having uttered such an infamous suggestion, which he had only done to tease his companion, and not thinking for a moment that there was really any substance in the idea, the bounty hunter said, 'Ah, don't take on so. I was only joshing with you.'

Had Judd but known it, he was closer at that moment to death than he had ever been before in the whole course of his life, even taking into account all the hair-raising situations into which his chosen career had led him. It would have taken very little to persuade Morgan to squeeze the trigger and be damned to the consequences. But the moment passed, and he knew that if he hadn't shot Judd in hot blood, he couldn't do it now that his fury had cooled and abated somewhat. He holstered his piece, contenting himself with remarking, 'You run your mouth reckless like that again and there's no telling where it will end, you take my meaning?'

'Surely. What say we set down now and reason together, figure out the best way of going about this here?'

Morgan did not answer for a few moments, but looked into the other's eyes, trying his best to gauge how likely this man would be to play him false. Very likely indeed, was the inescapable conclusion. Joshua Morgan was very far from being an educated man, and hadn't even a passing acquaintance with any works of philosophy or ethics, but the way in which he fathomed out the case in his own mind would have been only too familiar to many of the great thinkers of antiquity.

His ruminations might be summed up as follows: returning that boy to his mother was a good aim, and whatever he had to do in support of that purpose would be made right because of the ultimate goal. In

short, Morgan persuaded himself that the end justi-
fied any means used in accomplishing what he had
set out to do. It was a dubious philosophy viewed in
strictly ethical terms, but it satisfied him in the situation in which he was presently placed.

CHAPTER 6

One fact, or supposed fact, was working like yeast in
Morgan's mind as he and Judd trailed the Choctaw.
This was that the bounty man had been deceiving
him from the beginning, and had almost certainly
been planning to sacrifice Morgan's life as a means
of achieving his own ends. It took no great power of
brain to work that out. This in itself left Morgan ill
disposed towards the man with whom he had the mis-
fortune to be riding.

All of this served, at least to Josh Morgan, as justification for the plan that was now germinating in his
mind, to the effect that if anybody were fit to be used
and discarded as a way of ensuring that things went
smoothly, then it would better be Judd than himself.
The fact that he had no real evidence that Judd had
actually been fixing to throw him to the wolves so
that he could effect his own plans, was neither here
nor there. That look in his eyes had been all that was
needed to prove the matter for Morgan.

By the time they had been following the Choctaw for a couple of miles, Morgan had come to a decision. He still did not know definitely if Tommy was even with the people they were trailing, but if he was, then getting him free would require desperate measures. Since he believed that Judd had been prepared to sacrifice him for his own ends, Morgan had no compunction about planning a similar fate for his new partner. A verse from scripture came unbidden into his mind, lodged there years ago during a Sunday School lesson, perhaps: 'Whosoever rolleth a stone, it shall return upon him'. It summed up to a nicety how he felt about Judd.

They had not eaten since that morning and Morgan's belly was beginning to growl in protestation, when the bounty hunter suddenly announced that if it was all right with his partner, they could stop to eat a bite. He said this hesitantly, as though really prepared to abide by Morgan's decision. Whether this was because he respected him more for pulling his pistol and drawing down on him, Morgan didn't know, but there was a very real change in the other man's attitude towards him since the incident. Morgan said, 'I've nothing in the way of food. What about you?'

'Enough for the both of us, and you're welcome to share it if you will.'

In a way, it sat ill with Josh Morgan to sit down and break bread with a man whom he was planning to double cross should it prove advantageous, but he

was powerful hungry and this helped him to over-
come any scruples that he might otherwise have felt.
From somewhere, Judd had acquired a picnic meal
that he had stowed in his saddle-bag. There was a cut
of cold meat, cheese, rolls and apples. When the two
of them had finished, they lay back to digest the
food. There was no danger of losing the Indians,
there were far too many of them for that, and from
what Morgan had been able to make out, most had
been on foot. They were therefore proceeding at a
snail's pace. No, they could afford a little rest. Judd
rolled two cigarettes, lit them and· handed one to
Morgan. Then he said, 'Can't help thinking I might
have seen your face before. Any idea where that
might have been?

'You fought for the Confederacy?'

'Not hardly.'

'Then it wasn't during the war, I guess.'

'Maybe not. You surely look familiar though.'

All Josh Morgan's finely tuned antennae were
twitching now, for it seemed to him only too likely
that this wretch was hinting that he had recognized
him as a member of the Anderson Gang. The likeness that he saw on the wanted bill might not yet
have reached Texas, but there had been other such
bills circulated before. Did Judd think that he could
get a price for Morgan as well? The thought that this
might be so provided one more justification for
seeing if he couldn't get the bounty killer into a position where the Choctaw took care of him, which

would act as distraction and give Morgan himself a chance to snatch Tommy – always assuming that he was with their group.

As they mounted, preparatory to moving after the Indians, Morgan said, 'You got any notion on how we should be going about this, when night falls?'

'Well now, I got an ace in the hole, far as that goes,' said Judd with a wink.

'You're just full of surprises,' replied Morgan.

Taking this as a compliment, the bounty man smiled broadly and exclaimed, 'Ain't I just!'

'Go on then, let's be hearing about it.'

'See, I've a friend among those boys – though calling him "friend" is stretching the case a mite. Fellow I'm after is called Dull Knife. He's the chief's son and heir. His brother goes by the name of Running Wolf, though he's brother by another wife, so he's a half brother, call it what you will. Well, he hates Dull Knife. Wants him out the way, maybe so he can get in his father's good books, I don't know.'

'And this Running Wolf, he's the boy who'll hand over his brother to you, hey?'

'That's it.'

As the two men, the bounty killer and the one-time holdfast, set off again, they were both thinking how they might get the better over the other – though Judd had a distinct advantage in this field, for his whole life had been devoted to getting one over anybody with whom he had dealings. In his line of work, his very life depended upon this ability to betray anybody at the drop of the proverbial hat.

Judd Archer had guessed early on that Morgan was a wanted man. Why else would he be roaming across the Indian Nations in this way? He also figured that in reality, Morgan was after the reward money for getting Tommy Walters safely home. This made the other man a rival, though there was more to the case than that. Judd had a most remarkable memory, and having once glanced at a likeness on a wanted bill, it was indelibly imprinted upon his brain. He just knew when he first set eyes on the man asking after the boy he had lost, that here was somebody whose face he knew. The problem was that he could not put a name to the face.

Not having progressed beyond the most rudimentary schooling as a child, Archer's memory for the printed word was not as strong as his ability to recollect faces. Until he could recall just who this fellow was and where he had seen his likeness, there was no advantage in capturing him and so being obliged to transport two men and the boy back to Texas. This one might not be worth the trouble, and an extra pair of hands when raiding an Indian camp was always a good idea. This was why he had hinted at having seen the fellow before, to see if he could be alarmed into revealing his true identity. It was not until they mounted up after eating in order to head after the Choctaw that Judd Archer happened to notice two tiny letters burned into a corner of his partner's saddle: JM. As soon as he saw these letters it was enough to trigger the necessary memory: without a shadow of a doubt, this was a member of the Anderson Gang, Joshua Morgan! This was definitely a prize worth having.

Of course, word had not yet reached Texas, at least before Archer had set out for the Territories, about the robbery at Oakwood and the end of the Anderson Gang. But there was a thousand dollars payable for every member of the gang and the name of Morgan had been there, with an image of the man himself above it. The only fly in the ointment was that this reward was payable only on conviction. This would mean bringing the man in alive. Dull Knife was nothing, the bounty on him was dead or alive, and the boy Walters was unlikely to cause him any trouble. So it was now a question of when to take Morgan prisoner. One way would be to let him help in the capture of Dull Knife, and then after that not give any hint that he knew who he was riding with. That way, Morgan would ride back to Texas under his own steam and Archer could arrest him once they were safely back in civilization. But two things militated against such a scheme.

If there was one thing liable to irk Judd Archer, it was having a man pull a pistol on him. He had never yet backed down from any move of that kind and he was just raring to go, to show that young puppy that it had been a really bad idea to draw down on a stranger like that. The second point was that he did not trust this boy in any way, and thought it likely that given the opportunity, he might easily double-cross Archer himself. For both of these reasons, as the afternoon drew on, it became increasingly clear that he would have to act soon and ensure that Joshua Morgan posed no threat to him, but rather represented a tidy sum in cash money, which would be available as soon as a court had tried and condemned the man and caused him to be hanged.

As the red sun drifted down towards the horizon, there were signs that those they were following were stopping for the night. Morgan and Judd accordingly reined in as well and settled down to wait for darkness. They dismounted and walked about, stretching their legs a little, for they had been in the saddle since breakfast. Without breaking his easy walking pace, Judd Archer strolled over to his horse and said to Morgan, 'Come over here a moment. Got something I reckon you'd like to see.'

Curious to know what the man would show him, Morgan walked across to where Judd was standing by his horse and said, 'Well, what it is?'

From a scabbard at the front of the saddle, Judd withdrew a military carbine which nestled there. He wielded this with ferocious effect, striking Morgan sharply on the head with the stock. When the first blow proved ineffectual, he swung the weapon again. This time, Josh Morgan dropped senseless to the ground.

When Morgan came too, he found that he was lying face down in the dirt, with his wrists painfully lashed together behind his back. The man he knew only as Judd was sitting and smoking. When Morgan opened his eyes, he looked relieved. 'Thought I might've killed you there, son. You've a tough skull and no mistake!'

'What foolishness is this? Just untie me now.'

'I don't think it for a moment.' After explaining briefly to Morgan how he had discovered his true identity, Judd said, 'Problem is boy, I couldn't trust you, see. I could do with a little help in my next move, but there's no point in having you run around if you might do me harm. I'm sure you see that.'

'I killed a heap o' men in my time,' said Morgan, 'but that was in time of war. I never killed a man as wasn't wearing an enemy uniform.'

Judd Archer shrugged and asked without any particular interest, 'Why you telling me this? It's nothing to me.'

'To give you a chance. To let you know I killed as many men as you, and if you don't turn me loose right now, I'll kill you as well.'

'Don't see that!' replied Judd Archer, a smile playing on his lips. 'Why, it'll be all you can do to undo your pants so you can piss, conditions being as they are now. Can't think how you're a-goin' to kill me.'

All that Josh Morgan had seen of Tommy Walters in the short time that he had known him had led him to suppose the boy a fairly amiable, but not very adventurous or aggressive youngster. Truth is, he had him pegged for a mommy's boy. Indeed, the boy's own grandfather had hinted as much. But as it happened, there was more to the child's character than he had revealed, either to his grandfather or to the man who had been taking him home to his mother. Although he didn't care for scrapping, he had never allowed anybody to take liberties with him, and in his home town he had had a reputation for being a tough fighter. His father had taught him one or two tricks, but had impressed upon the child most forcibly that fighting was what you fell to when all other methods had failed. Only a fool went out looking for trouble – but only a coward ran when trouble reared its head.

Tommy had been alarmed when he was awoken in the middle of the night by a hand being clamped over his mouth, but he'd had the sense not to struggle or scream, but rather to wait and see where matters were tending. He had been carried off by two lithe young braves, who had watched the man and boy settling down to sleep that night. The Choctaw didn't go hunting for slaves, but when a healthy young boy like this showed up in their territory, then it was like a sign from the gods. They did not mistreat the captives whom they used as servants, and some had even grown up to be freed and become full members of the tribe. All that a boy like Tommy would need was food, and he could be used to carry burdens when they were on the move, and for gathering firewood, fetching water and a host of other tasks around the place when they were in one place. There were currently three other children in the same bind: two boys and a girl. They ranged in age from eight to fourteen.

The men who had taken him prisoner were not in the least cruel to Tommy. When they were clear of the spot where he had been sleeping alongside Josh Morgan, the man who had snatched him said softly, 'Make noise, get hurt!' Then he removed his hand from the boy's mouth and set him on his feet. Tommy kept silent, not because he was especially afraid, but rather because he had boundless faith in his friend Joshua. He sensed, without the least doubt or misgiving, that Morgan would come looking for him and set him free again. For now, he was content to bide his time.

One of the men hoisted Tommy Walters up on to a horse, so that he was sitting in front of the rider. Then they set off, to where he had no idea at all. After an hour or so, they arrived at what he took to be an Indian village. It was the hour before dawn, and there wasn't much going on. He was deposited on the ground with the warning 'Run, get hurt!' – and so he waited quietly until folk started waking up. After a bowl of thin gruel, consisting of parched corn mixed with a little cold water, Tommy was set to work with no more ado.

The work itself was not arduous, involving as it did just dismantling tents and helping carry bundles of poles from one place to another. He was treated rather like a beast of burden, though one with the advantage that he could learn and take instructions. When the Indians broke camp, he found himself carrying a pack that was not too arduously heavy. Nobody struck or abused him, and indeed, some of the women smiled at him in a friendly enough fashion. Nor was the pace of the march to a new location too fast for Tommy to manage.

Once they were on the move, the boy cast his eyes around in all directions, looking for any sign that the man who had promised to protect him was somewhere around. It wasn't until the middle of the day, when the sun was nearing her zenith, that Tommy saw in the far distance two dark specks which he could just discern to be men on horseback. It was too far to tell anything at all about these men, but he knew with an inner joy that one of them was his friend Joshua, and that he would spare no effort to rescue Tommy from the Indians. Even so, he knew that he would have to play his part, too. There was no point in just waiting for Joshua Morgan to come riding down and asking the Indians to relinquish their young prisoner. They might well refuse and just kill Joshua. No, he would have to take an active role in the business if there was to be any hope of him and Joshua resuming their interrupted journey back to his mother's home.

The day wore on, with only one halt, an hour or so after midday. These were hardy people, and even those with white hair seemed to have no difficulty maintaining the pace. There were travoises for transporting not only the tents and household goods, but also children too small to walk and too large to be carried by their mothers. When at dusk they stopped to make camp, Tommy found himself despatched with the other young slaves to gather firewood. The four of them were under the nominal control of a lame Indian boy who looked to be about fourteen years of age. Tommy thought that not only was this boy a gimp, he had the look about him of one who was a little slow on the uptake. At any rate, his face had a vacant and blank look about it.

When the foraging party was a good way from where the camp was being set up for the night, Tommy went up to the Indian boy and said, 'I'm a-going now, and I hope you won't be trying to stop me.' The boy to whom he spoke, in addition to having a withered leg, was also undersized and not a great deal taller than Tommy himself. He appeared to understand well enough the import of the words spoken to him, for he made a grab at Tommy, who had turned on his heels with the intention of leaving.

There was a short tussle, which seemed about to turn into a wrestling match. This was not at all to Tommy's liking, for if he was lame, the Indian was also muscular and lithe. Tommy broke free and then whirled round and landed a punch on the other boy's nose, causing him to stagger back, clap his hands to his face and squeal in pain. He stood there for moment and Tommy saw that blood was running down the fellow's chin. He said, 'Want any more? No? Well then, I'll be going.' He backed away warily, in case the Indian jumped him again, but there seemed to be no inclination on the part of the other to try conclusions a second time.

Before he could try and find Joshua, Tommy knew that he should hide up for at least an hour or so. He'd a notion that the Indians wouldn't search too hard for him – after all, they hadn't paid out money for him or aught of the sort. That being so, they might just accept it without too much fuss if he vanished again. They'd had a day's work out of him at any rate. He found a little rocky ledge beneath a towering oak tree, and here he secreted himself, sitting quietly to see if there was any hue and cry. In the gloom it was unlikely that even a wood-wise Indian would spot his whereabouts. After what he judged to be an hour was up and there was no sound of pursuit, Tommy Walters set off in the general direction of where last he had seen the two riders, one of whom he was convinced must be his friend coming to look for him.

Lying there in the darkness, Josh Morgan felt the bitterness of complete and utter defeat. The prospect of being tried and hanged was bad enough of course, but that he should have been taken by this crawling, slithering wretch whom he had not trusted from the start, that made the whole thing a sight worse. That he, of all people, should have been caught off guard by a man he knew to be a bounty killer, that was a bitter pill to swallow. The worst of it, though, was that he had failed in the promise he had made: to take care of that little boy and see him safe home to his ma. It was this failure that rankled most. Last night he had determined on a straight and honourable course of conduct, to take the child back to Springfield, even at hazard of his own life, and set him on the path home. Now, all his plans had come to naught and he was like to lose his own life into the bargain – by which it may be rightly judged that Morgan was feeling pretty sorry for himself as he lay in bondage.

The man whom Morgan knew only as Judd had fallen asleep, his mouth hanging open in the most vulgar and unbecoming way, as he emitted raucous snores. Morgan eyed the man with distaste and vowed to himself that if ever the tables were turned and the advantage lay with him, he would end the bounty-killer's life with no more compunction than he would feel in snuffing out a candle. It was while musing in this way that he gradually became conscious of a furtive rustling near at hand, as though some crafty animal were drawing nigh. Wondering if it were possible that this was a mountain lion or other dangerous beast, Morgan drew breath, with a view to shouting out to scare the creature away. He felt altogether helpless, laying there with his wrists bound behind his back.

But before Morgan had time to let out the deafening roar that he planned, Tommy Walters emerged from some nearby bushes and smiled shyly. The boy was plainly as pleased as Punch to see his friend again. The light of the full moon, pellucid and clear, shone down upon them, illuminating the scene almost as well as daylight. This was good, because it meant that when Morgan shook his head frantically at the boy, to indicate that he should not make any sound, Tommy was able to see the urgent look on his face and stopped where he was, standing stock still. He did not know what the nature of the danger was, but was fully alerted to the fact that Morgan wished him to proceed with the utmost caution. As he watched, the man lying on the ground puckered up his lips into what might have been the simulation of a kiss, but which Tommy correctly understood to mean 'Shush!' When Morgan jerked his head forwards a couple of times, Tommy again caught on that he was being invited to approach Morgan, although quietly. He tiptoed forwards until he was within earshot.

'Good boy,' whispered Morgan softly, 'My hands are tied. Think you can deal with the knots?'

Tommy squatted down and Morgan wriggled over on to his side, to allow the boy access to the thongs that bound him. He was in an agony of haste, fearing that at any moment the bounty man would awake and his hopes of freedom be dashed. So tightly pulled were the rawhide strips that it took the boy almost fifteen minutes to prise the knots free. By the time the thongs finally came loose, he was almost in tears of frustration.

As soon as his bonds fell free, Morgan experienced the most frightful pain in his hands, as the circulation was suddenly restored. This did not prevent him moving swiftly to where Judd lay slumbering. Propped up against a tree was Judd's rifle, and in addition to his own pistol in the holster at his waist, he also had Morgan's Colt tucked negligently in his belt. It was the work of a moment to take up the carbine and cock it. Then, holding it at his hip, Morgan leaned forwards and removed the two pistols, handing them to Tommy for safe keeping. Having done this, he lashed out with his boot, catching the sleeping man in his ribs.

Judd Archer was instantly awake and reached down for his pistol. His instincts had become so finely tuned over the years that he could be awake and ready for lively action in the merest fraction of a second. On finding that he was weaponless, the bounty-killer's eyes flicked over to the tree where he had left his rifle. Only when this, too, drew a blank did he lean back and see who it was who had the better of him. Watching his face when he realized who it was that was now drawing down on him was, thought Morgan, as good as a play. He said, 'What say I shoot you down now, you mangy scoundrel?'

Tommy gave an involuntary cry of horror and exclaimed, 'Oh, please don't hurt him, Joshua!'

The recollection of his allowing this child to see two men shot down and another beaten mercilessly around the head came to Morgan, and he felt a deep sense of shame. A fine guardian he had proved so far to this innocent young lad. It was not to be wondered at that Tommy was aghast at the thought of being compelled to witness more murder and mayhem. As he watched Judd's face, he could see the look of satisfaction at the discovery of a weakness in the man who was holding him at gunpoint. The temptation simply to squeeze the trigger was almost overwhelming, but Morgan knew that it might disturb the child for whose protection he was responsible. He said, 'You hear that, you crawling snake? This here child begs for mercy for you. You best recall in the future that the only thing that saved your worthless hide was a child's plea. I tell you straight, if it was the two of us here, I'd o' shot you without a second thought, same as I might stamp on a scorpion or such.'

'Then what?' asked Judd, 'You going to turn tables on me and bind me?'

Ignoring the question, Morgan said, 'You want to live, you'll do just precisely as you're bid, you hear me? Don't think I'll hesitate to shoot you, no matter what the boy says, if you try anything I don't care for.'

Despite this stern warning, Judd had a noticeably perky air about him now, being sure that Morgan was not going to shoot him out of hand. The truth was, he was mightily relieved that this was the case, because had the boot been on the other foot, he would surely have gunned down the man who had hog-tied him without giving the matter a second thought, no matter what some soft boy said.

Even at risk of upsetting Tommy, Morgan felt that a sending a ball through Judd's foot might deliver a wholesome message to the man on how to conduct himself in the future. But he knew that he was not going to do so, and instead said, 'You lie flat down on your face, and before God, if you move before I give you leave, I'll kill you. You know I mean it.'

Judd did as he was instructed, while Morgan, keeping an eye on him the whole time and the rifle at the ready, moved around, preparing the horses to leave. Before doing so, he had warned his young friend, 'You keep right over there out of the way, now. I don't want that damned reptile striking at you.'

When he was finished, Morgan's horse and Tommy's pony were ready to go. Judd Archer had taken his boots off before sleeping, and these Morgan picked up and placed in the saddle-bag on Judd's own horse. Then he instructed Tommy to mount up and told him, 'Walk your pony down a-ways to the bottom of the rise there. I'll join you directly.'

'You ain't going to. . . .'

'No, don't fret. Long as he stays lying there 'til we leave, I swear to you that I won't lay a finger on him.'

Trusting Morgan's word, the boy walked his mount down to where he had been asked, a distance of about fifty yards. Now that they were able to speak privately, Morgan said quietly to the man who was still lying flat on his face in the dirt, 'There was a time, not so long since, when I would have shot you for a fraction o' what you done. As 'tis, I aim to take your horse, guns and boots. You can make your own way back to Texas.' He was pleased to note that a look of sheer panic came into the prone man's face at this.

''Fore you utter one single word, I'll tell you one more thing. I lived my whole life long by the rattlesnake code. I'm guessing you heard of it, even if you scorn to abide by it. I never yet shot a man unawares, always gave notice of my intentions, never ambushed a man from behind. Well, there's exceptions to those rules. You know what I mean. When you're in pursuit of a man and he knows it, then he can lay traps for you, shoot you from cover, anything goes, so long as he knows that you're coming for him. Well, that's you. If ever I find you after this day, there'll be no warning. I'll shoot you before you even know I'm there.'

It seemed to Morgan that the man lying before him was minded to speak, but he didn't want to hear him. He said, 'I reckon you feel the same way about me, so we'll take that as it is. If ever we meet again, there'll be a reckoning.'

Before mounting up, Morgan coughed up phlegm and then spat on the bounty hunter. There was no response, and so he walked his horse away, leading Judd's alongside. As he made off, he kept a grip upon the rifle and twisted in the saddle so that he could see if the other man was about to jump to his feet and come running after him. But nothing of the sort happened, and even when he and Tommy set their horses at a trot, he glanced back and saw that Judd was still lying flat. The man was presumably dreaming up something particularly unpleasant that he would do to Joshua Morgan if ever their paths crossed again.

CHAPTER 7

It was only because the moon was so bright that Morgan was minded to undertake a journey of this sort at night. Even so, he intended that they should rest for a few hours and snatch a little sleep – though not until they were far away from the man whom he had left helpless. Tommy interrupted his thoughts to ask, 'Would you have done anything to that man if I'd not been there? Who was he?'

After giving a brief account of meeting the man called Judd and the circumstances that led to his falling into captivity, Morgan said, 'As to whether I'd a' hurt him, I can't say. Skunk deserved shooting is my private opinion, but what's done is written.'

'You been following me the whole time, since you found me gone?'

'Sure, what else? Didn't I say I'd see you safe back to your home? How'd you get away from them Indians, anyhow? I'm guessing that they did have you, meaning that band of Choctaw that me and the other fellow was trailing?'

Tommy then told the story of his escape from the Indians, which account caused Morgan to look with new respect upon his young friend. He said, 'You're something else again, you know that? You up and left by yourself and found me in the wilderness? But what if you'd got lost? Sooner we get you home to your ma, the better it'll be, I reckon.'

'What would you have done, then?'

'Same as you, I should think.'

They rode on for about two hours, sometimes at a trot and at others a walk. There might have been enough light, but Morgan was still scared of one of their horses setting a foot in a hole and breaking a leg in consequence. At last he said, 'Well son, we travel any longer and you're apt to fall asleep, tumble off your pony and break your neck. I think we've put enough distance between us and that scallywag. He's going to be walking barefoot, which will make for slow travelling.'

After they got down from their horses, Morgan untacked the bounty hunter's horse and turned it loose. The other two beasts, he hobbled. Tommy said, 'What will happen to that man? You think he'll be all right?'

'Born to be hanged will never be drowned,' growled Morgan. 'I dare say he'll survive, worse luck for the world. Men like him are a scourge.'

Before falling asleep, Morgan allowed himself another brief prayer, the one the previous night

118

having not quite done the trick as far as he could see. Once the boy was sound asleep, Morgan whispered the following, highly unorthodox petition to the Deity, 'Lord, I was going to take Tommy back to Springfield, but I don't think that'll answer, on account of there's a bunch of Choctaw in that direction who might try and take him again. Not to mention where there's also a most irate bounty hunter. No, I'll have to take my first plan, to head straight for Texas. I hope you'll watch over us and lend a hand where necessary, if not for me then for that child I have the care of. Amen.'

The following day dawned sunny and bright, although with a definite chill in the air, which presaged the arrival of winter. They'd no food, and so Morgan was forced to leave Tommy alone for a space while he went hunting. The rifle was a good one and he succeeded in taking down a brace of black-tailed jackrabbits. They weren't the largest game in the world, but they'd satisfy him and Tommy for now. It appeared that the idea of cooking and eating out in the open was a novel one to the boy, for he watched with great interest as Morgan kindled a fire and skinned and gutted the little animals. He said, 'How'll we manage without saucepans and knives and forks?'

'Just you sit back and watch, young fellow. Saucepans, indeed! Why, I never heard of such a thing when I was growing up!'

With a few green branches to skewer the jackrabbits, it took next to no time to broil them over the

119

fire. There was, as Morgan had assured him, no need for either knives or forks. They simply pulled the meat to pieces with their fingers, acquiring a few blisters in the process, but having the rare pleasure of eating tender flesh that had been alive and hopping around an hour earlier. They were both quite satisfied after the meal, and set off west in good spirits.

'How long will it take to get to Texas?' asked Tommy. 'I'm surely looking forward to seeing my ma again. I hope she hasn't been too worried about me.'

It hardly seemed the time, thought Morgan, to inform Tommy that from what he understood from the man called Judd, there was a general impression in Texas that Tommy was dead. It would be a grief to the child to learn that his mother might also be under this apprehension, and so he held his tongue, merely remarking cheerfully, 'Well boy, we'll have you home as soon as we're able, have no fear of that.'

All in all, it was a pleasant journey. There was no certainty where their next meal was to come from, but while he had a rifle at hand, Morgan wasn't really anxious on that score. By the time he was Tommy's age, Joshua Morgan had been out many a day hunting for the pot, and his life in the army had served only to sharpen his eye and improve his marksmanship. Starvation was the least of his worries. So far they had come across, and fallen foul of, bounty hunters and hostile Indians. He could not help but wonder what other perils might yet lurk unseen in the Territories. The only time he had previously been here was with an army, and visiting even the most unwelcoming area when you have a few hundred heavily armed men next to you is apt to blunt your sense of danger. He had felt the Indian Nations at that time to be no more hazardous than the farmland of West Virginia. The case was altered now, with just one wanted outlaw riding with a child. It was while thinking matters over in this way that Morgan noticed to his right, behind a range of low hills, what he at first took to be a column of smoke. Tommy also saw it and said, 'Something must be afire!'

After staring hard for a few seconds, Morgan realized that he had been mistaken, and observed, 'That's no fire. It's a body of riders. It's been a dry autumn and they're kicking up a whole heap of dust. Moving this way too, from what I can see.'

'Is it more Indians?'

'I couldn't say. Those hills are in our line of sight. Could be most anybody. We best get out of the way.'

Tommy looked sideways and said, 'Are you afraid?'

Morgan considered this question carefully and honestly, saying at last, 'No, I ain't afraid. But I have you to care for, young'un, which means I have to take more care about things than I might otherwise do.'

Tommy smiled slightly. It was plain that he was pleased to hear that somebody cared so much about him and was looking after him.

The country through which they were passing was

mainly grassy plains, but interspersed with tracts of woodland. There was one such afforested area nearby, and at Morgan's urging, they trotted their horses into it and made their way among the trees. When they were well out of sight of the path along which it seemed that the riders must come, Morgan told Tommy to dismount, doing the same his self. Then, after securing their horses to handy trees, he told the boy that he wished to see who was kicking up such a cloud. When he announced his intention of going to the edge of the wood to spy on the horsemen, Tommy begged to be allowed to join him, to which request he acceded. The two of them settled themselves down and waited.

To Morgan's immense surprise, the riders, when once they hove into view, turned out to be a troop of cavalry. 'Well I'm damned!' he muttered. 'What the deuce are those boys doing here?'

There were good grounds for Morgan's bewilderment at seeing this troop of the US Cavalry riding openly through the Territories in this way, as it was a flagrant violation of the treaty that had originally established the five civilized tribes in this area in the first place. All the five 'civilized tribes' had been deported here against their will on the assurance that if they remained within the boundaries set around their new territory, they would never again have cause to cross swords with the white man. Now, here were the army riding a coach and horses through the treaties and behaving as though they had a perfect right to be bearing arms here. When Morgan had been here with the Confederate army, it was quite a different case, because they had been in the Territories at the express invitation of the Cherokee.

The two of them, the young man and the boy beside him, watched as the thirty or so riders passed by at a distance not exceeding fifty yards. It was a fine sight. Only when the men were completely gone and even the sound of their hoofbeats had faded into nothingness did Morgan permit Tommy to stand up, observing, 'That's damned odd.'

'How so, sir? I mean Josh.'

'Army got no business here. Supposed to be Indian Nations.'

'I thought you said as you was here with the army during the war?'

'Yes, at the express wish of the Cherokee. They invited us in.'

'Were they on the rebels' side?'

'Rebels, is it, hey?'

'It's what my pa called 'em,' said Tommy defensively. 'I meant no harm.'

Josh Morgan grinned and said, 'Ah, you're all right. Some of us get a mite touchy 'bout that. But no, I wouldn't say that the Cherokee were exactly on our side. Weren't on anybody's side, on account of nobody is really on *their* side. They hate the bluecoats though, because of what happened twenty, twenty-five years since.'

123

'What was that?'

'You never hear tell o' the trail of tears?'

'I don't recollect.'

'Army, cavalry that is, drove all the Indians out of a large chunk of the south. Brought them here. Whole heap o' Cherokee died, chiefly old folk and little children. They never forgot it. Never forgave the bluecoats, what's more. If I was those boys we saw, I'd take care to stay clear of the Cherokee.'

Being a fairly ordinary kind of boy, hearing about what had happened to a bunch of people years before he was even born did not especially interest Tommy Walters. There was a more immediate matter that demanded his attention. He said, 'Where'll we find dinner? I'm coming on hungry.'

'You and me both. Let's ride on a-ways and see what chances. Those jackrabbits were tasty enough, but in truth, there's not overmuch meat on 'em.'

They rode on for another hour or more, through country that was slightly hilly and afforested in parts. At length they came to a rise of land which, when once they had gained the crest of it, gave them a glorious view of a grassy plain stretching to the distant horizon. And there, to Joshua Morgan's amazement and delight, grazed a small herd of buffalo. 'Well, will you look at that!' he exclaimed. 'There's a sight you don't see too often in more civilized parts of the country!'

'We don't have to walk through them, do we?' asked Tommy, 'They look kind of fierce.'

'No, we'll stampede them away from us. But first, I think we can solve the little problem of rations for a spell.' Dismounting, Morgan took up the rifle he had stolen from Judd Archer and stuck negligently in his saddle-pack. He worked the lever to bring a round into the breach and then lay on the ground to make sure that his aim was steady. The boy watched fascinated as the mighty beasts moved in a desultory manner across the plain, eating a few mouthfuls of the sparse vegetation and then moving on to the next tussock of grass.

Tommy Walters also got down from his pony and lay next to Morgan. He said quietly, 'You going to kill one?'

'You want to fill your belly, don't you? There's a good deal more meat in one of these creatures than in a hundred jackrabbits.'

The shot was shockingly loud in that peaceful and pastoral setting. The entire herd, consisting of something more than a hundred animals, began moving rapidly away from them, the thundering of their hoofs making the very earth vibrate, so that Tommy could feel the shaking against his belly as he lay prone. The noise of the shot echoed and rolled back and forth like a peal of thunder. One of the buffalo did not follow its fellows, but stood still for a moment, before keeling over and lying still.

Morgan got to his feet and in a leisurely and unhurried way, replaced the carbine in the rolled blanket at back of his saddle. Then he and Tommy led their horses down the slope to where the dead buffalo lay. As they walked, he said, 'It's an uncommon thing to see herds like that these days. Only reason they survive here is 'cause the Indians only take what they need of them.'

'You mean they only kill 'em to eat?'

'Not just eating, you know. They use them beasts for just about all their needs.'

'Don't see as a dead animal's good for much, 'cept eating.'

'Huh, spoken like a good, city-bred fellow. You never ask yourself what the tents was made of, the ones those Choctaw live in who snatched you? The clothes they wear? The needles they sew them clothes with? What their tools is made of? How they build their cooking fires?'

Tommy said nothing, suspecting rightly that no answer was needed or required to these questions. As they neared the dead buffalo, Morgan continued, 'The skins of the things, they use for their tepees. Make clothes out of it as well. They make a lot of things from bone, like their needles. Then there's ropes, made out o' skin too. Rawhide, you know. They saw off the horns and make cups and suchlike from those. Nothing's wasted.'

Once they reached the buffalo that had been shot, Tommy was astounded at the sheer size of the thing. He said, 'I reckon most of the meat will go to waste.'

'Can't be helped. At least we're killing from need. It's not like those damned fools who shoot them

from trains for the sport of it and just leave the car-
casses rotting on the plains. They kill thousands so,
and all to no good reason.'

Morgan pulled out the knife that he kept hanging
out of sight, in a sheath hanging at the back of his
belt, and began slicing into the animal. It took him a
good half hour to cut out fourteen pounds or so of
lean and wholesome meat. Having accomplished
this, he remarked, 'This should stave off our hunger
pangs for a day or two!'

'How shall we cook it?'

'Same way we ate them jackrabbits. We'll broil it.'

They divided up the meat, so each carried half,
and then made their way back up to the top of the
ridge, where a few straggly trees stood. Tommy said,
'I don't see much in the way of firewood. Only a
couple of dead branches and a few twigs.'

'We'll soon make that right. Scoot on back down
there and bring me as much buffalo shit as you can
carry. Only the dry stuff, mind.'

'Buffalo shi . . . I mean dung? For why?'

'Just do it and you'll see.'

Much of the black dung was greasy and foul, but
there was also plenty which seemed to be tinder dry
and light. The boy gathered up an armful of this and
took it back to where Morgan was kindling a small
fire with a few twigs and a little dry grass. He said to
Tommy, 'Just drop it down here and watch.'

To his amazement, Tommy saw that the dried
dung was combustible and burned as readily as wood

– better, in some ways, for the flames were fierce and had a bluish tinge to them. When he had fetched some more of the strange fuel, Morgan set to and held chunks of the raw meat above the flames with a green stick he had twisted from a nearby tree.

The two of them ate ravenously until their bellies were quite full. After sitting for a while and allowing the food to settle a little, Morgan said, 'We best be making tracks. I want to get you out of this area as soon as may be.'

'I thought you said the Indians were all at peace?'

'So I did, but that was before I saw that army patrol. The good Lord alone knows what they're about. Could be trouble in the wind.'

There was still some food left over, and before they rode across the plain, Morgan delved into the dead buffalo and produced a glistening slab of what he said was the liver. 'Best part of the lot,' he declared, 'We'll have this for our evening meal with the remainder of the meat.'

'I could surely do with some bread to go with it.'

'Well, there's none such, so we'll just have to make do with what we do have.'

The afternoon was overcast and grey, although there was, mercifully, no indication of rain. The gun-metal colour of the sky suggested to Morgan that autumn was soon to give way to winter, and he was glad that they were not heading north. The weather here was cool, rather than chilly, but even so it would only be a week or so more before sleeping out of doors became something of a trial.

They halted for the night a little before dusk. Morgan was reasonably tired, but he could see that the boy was bone weary and about at the limit of what he was able to do, without falling asleep in the saddle. Because he was used to driving his own self hard, Josh Morgan feared that he had pushed the child more than was healthy, and so determined that the next day would be a more relaxed one, with plenty of rests and not too long in the saddle at any one stretch.

They made camp that night in a little copse of aspen trees, with more than enough leaf litter and dead wood lying around so they were not compelled to fall back upon the use of excrement to fuel their fire. There was enough meat for another good meal, but Morgan took the big, slippery slab of liver from where he had stowed it in his saddle-bag. It was dusty and a little travel stained, but he brushed it off as best as he was able, and then proceeded to cook it slowly over the fire. When it was done to his satisfaction, he astounded Tommy by taking his powder flask and sprinkling gunpowder over it, remarking as he did so, 'This is the only seasoning needful to bring forth the flavour from this beauty!'

'Gunpowder! Surely it won't be fit to eat?'

'Just wait 'til you taste it, boy. Then tell me so.'

The liver tasted quite exquisite, different from any other food that Tommy had ever encountered in the whole of his young life. The gunpowder did, as

Morgan had hinted, add an indescribable piquancy to the meat. Although he never in later life used such a condiment, Tommy Walters never forgot how delicious that meal had been. Almost as soon as they had eaten, both Morgan and the boy realized just how tired they were, and after arranging themselves, fell into a deep and dreamless slumber, which lasted for Morgan until the small hours of the morning; but when he awoke it was with an inexplicable feeling of dread.

Josh Morgan lay there in the pale starlight for a space, wondering what might have awoken him. Overhead, the Milky Way shone like a handful of diamonds scattered upon a black velvet cloth. He was aware that he needed to make water, but not to such an urgent extent that this alone would have awakened him. After wandering away from where the boy was sleeping peacefully, Morgan relieved himself, and as he did so, became aware of a reddish glow in the sky to the south-west – in other words, in the same general direction that they would be travelling the next day.

Staring hard, he tried to make out if it was perhaps a bunch of campfires, or maybe something in the nature of a wildfire. The season had without doubt been plenty dry enough for such a thing over the last month or two. It was then, as he strained his eyes in the darkness, that Morgan heard on the very edge of his conscious mind, the sound of human voices. They were very far off and in the same direction as that odd glow, but it seemed to him that he could hear shouting and yelling of some kind. Uneasy in his mind over what this might portend, he went back to Tommy and lay down next to him again, soon drifting off himself.

CHAPTER 8

When they ate the next morning before setting off on the day's travels, it was plain that both Tommy and Morgan were heartily sick of a diet consisting of nothing more than broiled meat. Tommy said, 'You think we'll find something else to eat today?'

'I couldn't say,' replied the man absentmindedly; 'I guess we'll just have to wait and see.' Morgan was running over in his mind what he had observed during the night, and pondering upon the advisability of changing their route somewhat. The difficulty in that scheme was that there were mountains to the north and south, and any detour might entail climbing them, which was anything but an enticing prospect. In the end, Morgan figured they might as well keep on their current track, although he would be keeping an extra sharp lookout for anything unusual ahead of them. He said nothing of this to Tommy, for fear of alarming him needlessly.

It was not until they had been proceeding for

some two hours that Morgan discovered what had been behind the curious light in the sky, and also the faint shouting he had heard. For some little while he and Tommy had observed birds circling in the sky ahead of them, and from time to time, one of the birds would drop like a stone and vanish from sight. They were vultures, and in Morgan's experience, flocks of vultures were seldom harbingers of good fortune – and so it proved in this instance. As they neared what looked to be the focus of the birds' interest, a faint, tangy smell assailed their nostrils. At first Morgan took this to be the trace of woodsmoke from a fire, but there was also a hint of burned meat in there somewhere. A narrow stretch of woodland lay ahead of them, and the track they were following wended its way through this.

'Hold up,' said Morgan, 'Just rein your pony for a minute.'

Doing as he was bid, Tommy asked nervously, 'Is something wrong? Why do you want to stop?'

Morgan gave the boy a queer look and said, 'I lived through the whole of the war, some of the liveliest fighting you ever saw or heard of. Sometimes surviving it was just chance, but then again, I always had a cautious streak. Never was one to go blundering in without thinking through the consequence of it.'

They sat there quietly on their mounts for a minute, while Morgan listened and thought. At last, he said, 'I don't believe there's anybody around or ahead of us, but I'm going to have this rifle in my hands, cocked and primed, when we ride through yonder wood. That being so, I'd be glad if you could keep a steady pace to the rear of me. I don't want you getting caught in the crossfire if anything happens.'

The two of them, the man leading the way, rode slowly and carefully through the wood. They were not troubled, however, and emerged on the other side ten minutes later and none the worse for their experience. Having persuaded themselves that all this care had been quite unnecessary, when they did come upon the horror that soon assailed them, it struck them all the more forcibly, because by the time they had passed through the wood unmolested, they no longer had any apprehension of danger.

Before them, twenty yards or so from the trees, lay the remains of an army camp. It had almost certainly been established by the column of riders whom they had seen heading this way the day before. At an estimate there had been tents enough for thirty men, and there were about that number of corpses lying scattered amongst the charred remnants of their temporary base. All the tents had been reduced to ashes, along with anything else that would burn. It was now that Morgan understood the odd, lingering odour that he had detected mingled in with the smell of charred wood: a few of the dead soldiers had ended up lying in fires, and as their flesh roasted and burnt, it sent on the wind a ghastly fragrance, redolent of barbecues.

For Morgan, who had seen some pretty horrible

things during the war, the scene was grim enough, but for little Tommy Walters, it was like a terrible nightmare come to life. He gazed in bewilderment at the field of death, and found suddenly that he was retching and his mouth filling with bile. He somehow got down from the pony, staggered a few yards and then fell to the ground, vomiting up the remains of the liver meat they had eaten for breakfast. Morgan remained seated, his face stony. He was less affected by the death of these men, and his only real consideration was how the presence of hostile Indians in the area was likely to interfere with his mission of returning the youngster to his home.

It was only when he had dismounted and began wandering through the destroyed encampment that Morgan discovered that not all the corpses had yet stopped breathing. He was mainly looking for anything in the way of foodstuff, so that he and Tommy might vary their diet a little. Some bread would have been welcome, and he could not believe that every morsel of food would have been looted and removed by the Indians, who had evidently attacked the camp. To this end, he began turning over bags and boxes – those that had not been consumed by the flames, that is – with his foot. It was while engaged upon this task that he heard a husky cough, and for a moment his heart seemed to stop beating. Then he looked down and saw that what he had taken for just one more bloody corpse was actually a gravely injured man, covered with blood and, if Joshua Morgan knew aught of such things, not long for this world.

Squatting down by the side of the wounded man, Morgan said quietly, 'How you feeling, fella?'

'Not so fine,' admitted the man, with an attempt at a grin, 'Fact is, I ain't feeling too good at all.'

Morgan cast a swift and practised eye over the badly mauled body, and wondered that he was still in the land of the living. He said, 'You thirsty? You want that I should get you some water?'

'That's right kind of you. I thank you.'

Morgan walked over to his horse and fetched the canteen that hung there. Tommy appeared to have recovered to some extent, and, interested to see what Morgan was about, followed him over to where the wounded man lay. After Morgan had let him slake his thirst, the man said, 'I knowed this was a fool's errand, before ever we started out on it.'

'The errand being what?' asked Morgan.

'Why, to show the flag, as the captain had it.'

'If it wouldn't tire you too much, I'd sure like to know more about this. I'm taking this lad through the Territories, see, and I'd like to know of any hazards.'

'Happen it'll tire me, but that's nothing to the purpose. I been lying here alone since last night, I want to talk. After we finished with the Southrons and done away with slavery there, there's only one corner of the country where it still goes on.'

'Meaning in the Indian Nations?' asked Morgan. 'I knew that some of the tribes here kept slaves, but I guess I thought it was all done away with when the war ended.'

'Not a bit of it. Mind, I think that's what you call an excuse.'

'How so?'

'Could you favour me with another swig from your canteen?'

After the soldier had drunk some more, he seemed breathless and agitated. Morgan assumed that the pain was getting to him, and perhaps he was scared of death. Still and all, he had no morphine to dull his agony, and he wasn't a padre and so could not reassure him about heaven and so on. Instead, he just waited quietly, to see what the fellow would say next.

'See,' said the man at length, 'I think the government wants this here land back again, and they're a looking for a reason to take it. We been told to ride patrols through here, like it's enemy territory.'

Morgan said, 'I don't know what we can do for you, truly. We don't have a spare mount and it looks to me like whoever attacked you took every horse.'

'That they did. We camped here last night, and they fell upon us at midnight or later. Hollering and whooping and killing every one of us.'

''Cept you.'

'You got eyes in your head. They killed me too. I just ain't stopped breathing yet, is all.'

This was such a neat and pithy summing up of the case, that it seemed to Morgan pointless to dispute with the fellow about it. He had been hacked about and partly burned on one side and the miracle of it was that he was not yet dead. Presumably in the haste of their attack the Indians had not bothered to go round the field of battle, checking every individual body for signs of life.

'There's one thing you can do for me,' said the soldier, 'If it wouldn't be asking too much.'

'Whatever it is, I'll try and oblige.' Said Morgan.

'I'm mortal afraid of being left out here for the animals to chew up and pull to pieces. If you would engage to see that I'm buried decent, I'd die easier.'

'You have my word on it. We'll stay with you to the end, and then I'll make sure that you're not left out here in the open. Even read a prayer over your grave if that'll comfort you.'

The man managed a feeble smile at that and said, 'I've not been one for church. Doubt the Lord'll be impressed by a few prayers at this late stage.'

They stayed with the cavalryman for most of that morning. As the pain increased, the weaker he grew, and he did not talk much after that long conversation. At a little before midday he breathed his last, which was a great relief for Morgan, who desired to leave as soon as he was able, in case those who had massacred the patrol returned. He had managed to scavenge the better part of a loaf of bread and some cheese as well, from provisions that seemed to have been overlooked. Everything else – horses, food, guns and any other equipment – had all been carried off. What they had not taken had been burnt.

Once he was sure that the fellow was dead, Morgan said, 'Come on, we need to be leaving. Half the day's been wasted already. It's a damned nuisance.'

Tommy Walters stood stock still and stared at Morgan in amazement. He said, 'We're going to bury him first though, aren't we? You know, on account of what he told us about being afeared as some animal might ate him up or something. You made a promise.'

'I did it to ease his passing. I'd no intention of keeping my word.'

The look in the boy's eyes was a reproach to Morgan. He felt called upon to further justify his actions, saying, 'It's the living as matter in this case. Any moment, some band o' savages might descend upon us and cut us to pieces. I promised your grandpa I'd get you home safe.' As soon as he'd said it, he knew he'd made a false move.

'Yes, you promised grandfather and he's dead, but you'd keep your word to him. Strikes me you make promises that you don't keep.'

'You're a child. You know nothing of such things. Mount up now, we're leaving.'

He'd no intention of owning it in front of the boy, but the truth was that Morgan did feel a little mean about having promised a dying man something, and then reneging on his word as soon as the fellow breathed his last. Even so, he felt he was in the right, for there was a living boy in the case, whose very life might be cast into jeopardy if they lingered too long in one area of these godforsaken parts.

After they had been riding in silence for some good long way, Morgan said suddenly and unexpectedly: 'I like you, Tommy. I like you more than I did that grandfather of yours, and more so than that dying stranger. I don't want harm to befall you. If I have to break promises or hit men or even kill them to take you to safety, then I'll do it.'

Tommy made no immediate answer to this heartfelt declaration, but after a minute or two, he said, 'I guess I never seen the real world before. I only known such things from storybooks. The things I seen since leaving my grandpapa's house, it's not how things are in books.'

'You got that right. If I'd've lived my life like somebody from a Sunday School story, I doubt I'd be here today to tell the tale.'

Although he sensed that Tommy Walters was still shocked and a little disgusted at the casual way in which he had broken his pledged word to a dying man, the atmosphere seemed to Morgan a little lighter after this brief exchange, for which he was thankful.

They saw no sign of Indians or anybody else as the afternoon passed. Morgan was ticked off with the cavalry for stirring up a hornets' nest: just when he was himself trying to pass peaceably through the Indian Nations they would have to set upon such a foolish course of action now, when he had almost got the boy safe to Texas. When Tommy asked what the army were really up to, he was happy to give his own interpretation of events.

'We had a man in my regiment, he was as educated as you like. Spoke Latin and Greek and Hebrew and I don't know what all else. Lord knows what he was doing enlisting as an infantryman. Anyways, he said that there allus had to be what he called a "Casey's belly", or some such name – it means a reason for fighting, to start a war or what have you.'

Tommy Walters' face brightened and he said, 'Hey, that old tutor of mine tried to teach me about that very thing, not long 'fore I runned away! It's called a cassis belli – Latin, I think he said. Means cause of war, don't it?'

'What it is to have an education! Yes, I reckon that's what it was. Anyhows, sometimes folks have to hunt around for such a thing, a reason to fight, and if they can't find anything fitting, then they can make one up out of nothing. I should say that's what we saw back there, with them cavalrymen as was massacred.'

Morgan paused for a while, in order to marshal his thoughts. Then he continued, 'I'd say it suited somebody well to have that patrol wiped out. Gives them a chance to come into these here Territories in force and break the fighting power of the tribes. Having a bunch of men killed like that will get everybody worked up about what a dreadful thing it was. Truth is, they must have known that thirty men would be

141

outnumbered ten to one if they ventured into the Indian Nations. Now they can go on about what a tragedy it all is and how they want to free the slaves here, and a whole heap of high falutin' stuff. What it's really about is land. It's what all wars are about, when you come right down to it.'

This discussion, in which Tommy had been able to contribute his own knowledge, set a more pleasant and agreeable tone for the afternoon, and served to banish the ill feeling that had been in the air. By the time they stopped for the night, Morgan and the boy were good friends again. By Morgan's reckoning, they might cross into Texas the following day and be in Jubilee the day after that. It was a great relief to him to see the end of the journey in sight.

They were on distinctly short commons that evening, with only a crust of bread and a little cheese that had seen better days. Both of them slept well, though, despite their bellies not being overfull. But it wasn't until he opened his eyes the next morning that Morgan realized that the renewed friendliness between him and Tommy Walters had caused him to relax and lower his guard at precisely the wrong time, because sitting on the ground watching him was the bounty hunter whom he knew only as Judd.

'Lordy, you was slumbering like a child,' said the bounty hunter cheerfully, 'I hardly liked to waken you. Took the precaution of removing your gun, though. Hope you don't mind.' He had a pistol in his hand, which was cocked and aiming straight at

Morgan's face.

Hoping to get a little closer to Judd, perhaps close enough to cut his throat with the knife that he still had in the sheath at his back, Morgan made as if to sit up. Judd said in the same agreeable tone, 'You sit up and you're a dead man. Just lie there now and I'll tell you how we will play this. I ain't taking a single chance with you.'

It struck Morgan that this man certainly intended to kill him, of that there could not be the slightest doubt. Morgan's guess as to why Judd had not simply murdered him while he slept was that he wished to crow about his cleverness. This proved to be an accurate summation of the situation, for the bounty man said next, 'I guess you wonder how I managed to recover my fortunes and get here to ambush you?'

'Well, you want to tell me.'

Tommy had now woken up and was watching fearfully, wondering what was going to happen. Without taking his eyes off Morgan, the bounty killer said, 'You don't need to fear, boy. I mean you no harm. Fact is, I want to get you safe home every bit as much as you want to get there. More so, maybe, for it's worth a chunk of cash money to me to get you back to the bosom of your family.'

'Can I get some water from yon canteen?' asked Tommy nervously, 'I'm powerful thirsty.'

'You go right ahead. I don't fear you. It's this one here that I have to treat like a rattler.'

'You were going to tell how you managed to get

back on your feet,' remarked Morgan casually. He had no idea of how he would manage to reverse the predicament in which he now found himself, but as long as he was alive, there was a chance of doing so. Tommy was swigging from the canteen and looking scared. It was hardly to be expected that a child could help him out of this fix, and Morgan knew deep down that if he was to free himself of these coils, then he would have to rely entirely upon his own efforts.

'As for that,' said Judd Archer, 'It was simplicity itself. I always have a little muff pistol tucked into my boot, just for a reserve. If you'd not been so careful last time we met, I might've been able to shoot you in the back as you were leaving, but you never once took your eyes off me.'

'Just as well, I should say.'

'Yes, but that Derringer, it's only good at close range. It's a two-five calibre and no barrel to speak of. Anyway, I trudged along the trail, looking as sad and broken-spirited as could be – and guess what? A white man rode by and stopped when he saw me. Wanted to help.'

'I can guess the rest of that tale easily enough,' said Morgan, 'You waited 'til he was close enough and then you shot him and stole his boots, guns and horse.'

'I did. You know, you and me, we ain't so different really. We understand each other real good.'

It was on the tip of Morgan's tongue to issue a

furious denial to this statement, but two things prevented him from doing so. The first was that it would be reckless to annoy a man who was probably intending to kill him shortly. The second was that when he considered the matter, he was forced to concede that there might be something in the notion.

Judd began talking again about the cunning way in which he had worked out the likely route that Morgan and the boy would be taking to Texas, and it was as plain as a pikestaff that he was boasting and just wished others to acknowledge how clever he had been. Morgan made appropriate sounds of appreciation as a way of keeping the man jawing away, but while doing so he was appalled to see Tommy pulling the carbine from Morgan's saddle and using the lever to cock it. He wanted to shout a warning to the boy and tell him to put the gun down and leave it alone. He knew, though, that should he do so and Judd saw that Tommy had the rifle in his hands, he would most likely open fire instinctively. So, he tried to keep the man's attention on him, saying, 'What happened about that Choctaw that you were aiming to take, with the help of his brother?'

'Well, now that you mention it, that's another crow I got to pluck with you. 'Cause I didn't have a horse or a gun, I couldn't take him. You cost me a load o' money there, a whole load.'

From what Morgan could make out, Tommy Walters had cocked the carbine, and it was now ready to fire. He was pointing it in the bounty killer's general direction, but the way he was holding it, it would kick like a mule and the ball would be apt to fly anywhere at all – even at Morgan himself. But then Judd, either because he suddenly had the thought that the boy who had begged permission to fetch a drink was taking the deuce of a time about it, or perhaps maybe because he had caught the glint of interest in Morgan's eyes – for whatever the reason, Judd glanced behind him, and seeing a gun in somebody's hands, began to whirl round, with the intention of killing the boy who held it.

Then everything happened with great speed. Morgan called out in alarm, hoping to distract Judd and prevent him from killing the boy. As soon as the bounty killer's attention was on Tommy and away from him, Morgan sat up and reached for his knife. Tommy, suddenly panicking, inadvertently squeezed the trigger of the rifle he was gripping, and the ball struck Judd Archer in the back. The shock of this caused Archer in turn to fire his pistol, as a reflex tightening of the muscles consequent upon the shock of a bullet hitting him in the region of his spine. Joshua Morgan felt a sharp burning sensation in his shoulder and knew at once that he, too, had been shot. This was of little import, though, because he also knew that unless stopped at once, the man he knew as Judd would kill Morgan and Tommy both.

Morgan pulled the knife free of its sheath and leapt at the bounty killer. The ball he had received must have shaken Judd Archer, for he hesitated fatally for a moment, unsure whether the chief danger came from the boy with the rifle or the man flying at him with a knife in his hand. It was a perfect example of that wise old saw which suggests that those who hesitate are lost, for Josh Morgan took full advantage of the split-second delay to slash his knife across the other man's throat. Having cut through the main blood vessels once, he put as much force as he could into a second, sweeping arc, which almost removed the bounty killer's head from his shoulders. Just to be sure, Morgan kicked the pistol from his hand, too.

The whole episode, from when Judd Archer turned to see what the boy was about, until he slumped to the ground, bleeding like a stuck hog, took the merest fraction of a second. Scarcely glancing at the man whose throat he had cut, Morgan dropped the knife and hurried over to where Tommy Walters stood, aghast at the bloodbath he had precipitated. He said, 'You're shot. Your arm is all over blood.'

By now, Morgan had realized that the ball had just nicked the biceps of his upper arm – it was barely a flesh wound. He said, 'Are you all right, son?'

'I guess. I didn't mean for to shoot him. I just wanted to scare him into letting us go.'

'You barely touched him, Tommy. It was me as did for him. If I hadn't cut him, your shot would have troubled him no more than a gnat bite. His death is upon me, but that's fine. I should've killed him last time our paths crossed. No matter. You're truly feeling all right?'

'I guess. . . .'

'Listen, you set down here for a little and recover yourself. And hand me that weapon, I don't want any more shooting.'

After the boy sat down, looking a little pale and shaky, Morgan went over and examined the corpse of the late bounty killer and established to his own satisfaction what he had already suspected: that Tommy's random shot had inflicted a mortal wound on the man, and he would have died within a short while even if Morgan had not cut his throat. There was no earthly reason to tell the child this, and Morgan felt it far better that Tommy should believe that all responsibility for the death lay upon the shoulders of another.

Severing the neck of the bounty man had sprayed blood all around, and it had stained even the blanket in which Tommy Walters had been wrapped during the night. Morgan did his best to clean up a little, but his own clothes were also bedaubed with the dead man's blood. It seemed to him that the sooner they left the scene, the better it would be for the boy, because this was a hell of a thing for him to have seen. Morgan bound up his arm where the ball had just grazed it, but it soon stopped bleeding. All in all, there had been some lucky escapes for everybody, except the man called Judd.

Tommy was exceedingly subdued that morning,

and try as he might, Morgan could do nothing to raise his spirits. He was fascinated by the death of the bounty hunter in a way that he had not been when Morgan had shot and killed the two men soon after they had left his grandfather's home. Perhaps it was because he had been more intimately connected with the business this time – not to mention that he had actually met Judd, and knew him not as a mere cipher, but an actual human person. Then again, there was the manner of his death. Few people, even grown men and women, are able with complete equanimity to watch a man having his head almost removed from his body. Whatever the reason, the journey that day was a sombre one.

CHAPTER 9

Before they slept, Josh Morgan had calculated that there were but thirty miles or less to go before they reached the border with Texas. He had hoped that it would have been possible to have travelled that distance on that day, but after the morning's events, this was doubtful. Tommy was looking anxious and low – as well he might after such a dreadful experience. On top of it all, there was not a scrap of food on which they could break their fast. This circumstance alone made for a subdued mood.

Morgan was not, in general, one for believing in miracles, but when they encountered a lone traveller less than hour after they had set off, frying sausages in a pan over a fire, even he was inclined to thank providence. The man looked old but hale, and as they approached his camp he called out in a cheery voice, 'You boys hungry? Eating alone's a sad business, and I could do with company.'

As though in a dream, they reined in by the

stranger's camp and dismounted. The man was clad all in black and carrying no visible weapon, which prompted Morgan to enquire, 'You a priest or something?'

'Missioner. These folk hereabouts are what you might call my flock.'

'We can pay for any food you share with us.'

The fellow gave him an odd look and said, 'You think I'd charge a fellow being for sharing of my vittles? You're a strange one, son, and no mistake. Where you headed?'

As he talked, the old man brought out a loaf of bread and some more sausages. The three of them ate heartily, and when they were replete, Morgan said, 'We're right thankful to you sir. I don't know what we'd have done had we not come across you.'

'I'm guessing that you know there's trouble in the wind,' said the old man, waving away Morgan's thanks with a gesture of his hand, 'I can't think what you're about, bringing a child here.'

'Yes, it was a false move, I'll allow. Do you happen to know how far the state line is from here?'

'Twenty miles or thereabouts, but I wouldn't trust a line on the map to protect you if the Cherokee are roused. They and the other tribes kind of regard the whole country as theirs, not just this little corner. Can't say as I blame them, neither.'

Morgan rubbed his unshaven chin thoughtfully and said, 'Are we like to meet any war parties 'tween here and Texas?'

'I couldn't say. The army have raised Cain with their foolishness. Anything's possible.'

'Are you heading out of the Territories?' asked Morgan. 'Maybe we could travel together. Might make for safety in numbers.'

'No, son. I'm heading in the opposite direction. I've just been visiting my family over in Texas and now I'm going back after my furlough.'

'You ain't afraid?'

'Ah, these boys are my children. I doubt they'd kill me. Still and all, you never know!'

They left the old missionary, very thankful for the meal he had provided them. As they rode off, Tommy said, 'You think he's in danger?'

'I'd say that's certain sure, but you can't help but admire a man who rides towards trouble, rather than fleeing in the opposite direction!'

'He was nice. I wish he'd've come with us. I hate to think of him being scalped or something.'

There was an anticlimactic feel to the day, as it seemed pretty certain now that they were out of harm's way. This made it all the more alarming when, soon after the sun had passed her zenith in the heavens, first one shot and then a ragged fusillade rang out from the hills to their left, and the man and boy found that a band of Indian braves were whooping and riding down on them. Morgan and Tommy were currently walking their mounts up a gentle rise, which Morgan hoped would allow them to see Texas when once they reached the crest. Morgan shouted at the boy to spur on his pony and rode alongside Tommy, to shield him from any stray shots. The Indians, whom he took to be Cherokee, were perhaps two miles off, but closing fast.

It was a bitter feeling for Morgan that having guided the boy safely through so many hazards, they should fall thus, within touching distance of their goal. Without slackening his speed, he drew his pistol, unsure whether he should turn and fire at the pursuers or simply shoot Tommy now to spare him whatever torments the warriors might be minded to inflict upon him. Things were very different now from when the Choctaw had taken Tommy into servitude. These braves had their blood up, and would be looking to cause as much suffering and death to any white folk as ever they were able.

It was obvious that Tommy's pony was struggling now to gallop up the slope, and both its laboured breathing and the white flecks flying from its mouth and nostrils were testament to the likelihood of the creature dropping down from exhaustion at any moment. The two of them gained the ridge – and there below them saw the most beautiful sight that ever their eyes beheld, for the plain was thick with tents and blue-coated soldiers. If only they could be alerted to the peril in which Morgan and the boy found themselves, they would surely rush to their aid. The only means of drawing attention was itself a dangerous one, but there was nothing else to be done. Morgan fired his pistol twice into the air and was instantly rewarded by seeing heads jerk in their direction. He only hoped that they would not identify him as a foe and respond by shooting down himself and his companion.

The men pursuing them were barely a quarter of a mile behind, and for some reason were not shooting at Morgan or Tommy. Probably, thought Morgan, because they hoped to take them alive, so that they could provide a little sport for their captors when they were tortured to death. The two riders began cantering down towards the cavalry encampment, and judging from the shouts and sudden burst of activity that could be observed below them, the soldiers had now seen how the case stood. Even though, Morgan could not fathom out at all why none of the men in the camp were firing yet. He found the answer when he and Tommy had gained the level ground. There then came a thunderous roaring – a continuous and unremitting wave of noise, the like of which he had never before heard in his life.

It was at this point that Tommy's pony gave up the ghost and toppled to the ground. Luckily the boy was nimble enough to leap clear, and so avoided being crushed when the unfortunate creature went over on its side. Looking back to see if they were still in danger, Morgan was amazed to see that every one of the riders who had been chasing them appeared to have been killed, along with their horses. Either there had been some stunningly accurate rifle fire, or there was some other explanation. He soon found out the truth of the matter, for at that moment the loud roaring ceased and there was an eerie silence.

The answer to the puzzle soon revealed itself when Morgan carefully scanned the camp they were nearing. He saw a gleaming brass and steel contraption, from which curls of smoke drifted lazily: it was a Gatling gun. He had heard of these weapons, but never before witnessed one in action. From what he understood, all that was necessary was for one man to keep turning a handle, and as long as ammunition was fed into the thing, a continuous fire was produced of bullets with a one-inch calibre. All that he had heard during the war did not do full justice to the fearsome ability of this deadly device, which could destroy an entire Indian war party simply by a single man working a crank, such as one would use to draw up a bucket from a well.

After dismounting, Morgan spoke quietly to Tommy, saying, 'I guess you've had about enough excitement to last your whole life long.'

'It's a real shame about my pony. He is dead, ain't he?'

Morgan crouched down and examined the animal. When he stood up, he said, 'I'm sorry to say he's no longer with us. Had you had him long?'

'Only since I been with my grandpa. He got him for me, like a present, I guess.'

'Well, leastways you ain't dead yourself, and that's something to be thankful for.'

An officer and two troopers came hurrying up to

where Morgan was standing with Tommy. He said, 'That was a close enough shave for you and the youngster. Another furlong and they would have had you, I think.'

'I'm deeply sensible of it,' said Morgan. 'And you've my thanks. We owe our lives to you.'

While Morgan was chatting to the captain, one of the men accompanying him was staring fixedly at Tommy, and eventually said, 'I'd say you're Tommy Walters from Jubilee. Am I right?'

'Yes, sir.'

'Lord God, your mother is still distracted with grief. Everybody thinks you're dead, you know. There's bills up with your likeness on them all over the town. Where the devil have you been all these months?'

'What's this, hey?' asked the captain. 'You the missing boy as all the fuss was made about?' He looked hard at Morgan with no friendly eye and said, 'You'd better have a damned good explanation for having that boy in your keeping, I'll tell you that for nothing!'

It took the better part of an hour to reason out the case to the satisfaction of Captain Trent. It appeared that the unit he commanded were normally based at Fort Williams, just a stone's throw from Jubilee. The disappearance of the little boy had been attributed variously to Indians, mountain lions and sexual maniacs; the reward offered had been a vain hope, and the universal assumption was that the child was dead.

'So you brought him safely home, all the way from Ohio, hey?' said Trent, a note of admiration in his voice. 'That's the hell of a thing. And you say this grandfather's dead now?'

'So I think.'

'Well sir, if anybody earned that reward, I should just about say that you had.'

'I don't want no reward for what I did,' said Morgan. 'Nothing of the sort. I'm not the one to care for that poor boy a minute longer. I taken him into danger, and it's no thanks to me that he's survived.'

Captain Trent stared long and hard at the young man standing before him, and guessed that there was more about this business than he was ever likely to know. Still, there was no doubt that this man had taken care of the missing boy as best he was able. He said, 'You say the boy's mount is done for. We got a train of wagons heading back to Fort Williams for supplies. They'll pass Jubilee on the way. What say you and the boy ride along of them?'

'If you give me your oath that you and your men will deliver him safely home, I reckon I can rest easy and will have fulfilled my pledged word. I don't think I'm good to be around for a young'un that age. Be a deal more wholesome for him to be in the company of your men.'

The captain looked at Morgan for a moment, and then stuck out his hand. He said, 'There's a lot more to this than I can guess, but I think you looked after that child as best you could. I promise we'll get him home safely to his mother.'

The two men shook and Morgan went off to find Tommy, who was having the mysteries of the Gatling gun explained to him. He said, 'Tommy, sorry to interrupt, but could I have the favour of a word?' When they were out of earshot of the others, he said, 'This is where you and me part company. You'll be safer with these boys than ever you was with me.'

'You ain't coming all the way to Jubilee?'

'I'm not.'

'I'll miss you. You said it would be rare fun sleeping out, and is surely was.'

'I led you into danger as much as I rescued you. I'm not the best influence on somebody your age.' At first he wondered if he should shake hands with the boy, or if that would be too formal, but Tommy decided the matter by throwing his arms around him and saying, 'I'll never forget you and the things we did.'

'Me neither.'

As he prepared to leave the army camp, Joshua Morgan reckoned matters up in his head and thought that he wasn't too far behind on the deal. He had kept his word to a dying man and seen the boy safely through a lot of difficulties. On top of which, he still had almost the whole of the three hundred dollars that Jacob Walters had given him. That should keep him going for a while, at any rate. As he rode away, he turned back to see if Tommy Walters would wave to him, but already the boy was engrossed once more in the Gatling gun, and didn't even look round to see when Morgan vanished from sight.